KAWARTHA CHRISTMAS CAPER

Gary Celdom Case Journals #4

By

Douglas J. McLeod

KAWARTHA CHRISTMAS CAPER

Gary Celdom Case Journals #4

McLeod, Douglas J. 1971 –

Kawartha Christmas Caper
Gary Celdom Case Journals #4

First Edition

ISBN-13: 978-1533642790
ISBN: 1533642796

1. Detective – Fiction.
2. Toronto (Canada) – Fiction.
3. Peterborough County (Canada) – Fiction.

Acknowledgements

First, and foremost, I would like to thank my darling wife, Catherine, for enduring my writing endeavors over the course of our relationship. She is my complete world, and I appreciate she's willing to put up with my insanity.

I would also like to thank my Aunt Pat, my mother, Penny, and my sisters and brothers, for supporting my hobby. It's hard to believe I've been at this game for five years when this book is first released, and I thank you for the love and support you've all given me during that time.

Finally, I'd be remised not to thank all of the crazy writers I've come across in my life. These are not limited to, but including, Jen F., Allison C., Laura S., Bethlyn B., Cassandra J., Crystal S., Sonya R., Dawn M., Barb J., Alice H., and many others I'm probably neglecting to mention. We're all a bunch of crazy writers, and I'm honored to be a part of their world.

Finally, thank you, the reader, for enjoying this wild ride with me. And, believe me, it's far from over.

Douglas J. McLeod

Other Books by Douglas J. McLeod

Scarlet Siege
Barbadian Backlash
Gary Celdom Case Journals: Volume One
Rouge Numbered Week

CHAPTER 1

I was sitting at my desk, pleading my case to my partner and girlfriend, Jessica Amerson, and was in the midst of losing.

"Oh, no," Jessica protested. "Absolutely not."

"Come on," I argued, "he has nowhere else to go."

"Gary," she stated, "I know he's your friend, but this was supposed to be a private getaway to your cottage for Christmas; just you, me, and Benny."

"Ahem," the ghost of my former fiancée, Karen Prairie, corrected. "I believe you're forgetting someone?"

"Sorry, Karen," Jessica corrected. "You, me, Karen, and my pet husky, Benny."

"I know," I replied. "But, Phil is going to be all alone for the holidays. Normally, he goes away to his aunt's up in Peterborough, but she's been fighting a bad cold, and doesn't want him to catch what she's got."

"What about Jim?" Jessica queried.

She wanted to push babysitting Phil off on his roommate, Jim Marsden. I had to explain, "He's gone to Vancouver to spend time with his family out there, and won't be back until just after New Year's. Can't Phil just tag along with us? I don't want him to be all alone, given his 'issues'."

She meant my best friend, Phil Bennett. We'd first met while on a case for the local NoMo writing challenge community. A few months later found us meeting up at the Northern Winds television series convention. We'd been best friends ever since. Around a year after the fan con slash hostage incident, Jessica and I found Phil loitering outside of an off-track horse racing betting place in the Beaches. That's when we learned about his compulsive gambling.

He'd been seeking treatment, going to therapy sessions near the University of Toronto for over a year before they kicked him out, a.k.a. 'graduated', from their program. Since then, Phil attended weekly therapy sessions. Still, I worried about him suffering a relapse and wanted to invite him up to my cottage with us. It'd remove him from all the Greater Toronto Area's triggering situations.

"Look, Gary," Karen interjected, "I can understand you're worried about Phil, but Jessica had her heart set on a private holiday getaway for you both. With your friend there, any chance for whatever romance she might have had planned will be thrown out the window."

"Thank you, Karen," Jessica appreciated.

"Um, not to nitpick here," I pointed out. "But, if the ghost of my departed fiancée is going to be lurking around the place, I think these alleged 'chances of romance' are going to be slim-to-none."

"Hey now," Karen objected, "I would do my part to make myself scarce if you two wanted to become intimate."

I blinked. "Jessica wants to be intimate?" I asked.

"Get your mind out of the gutter, Celdom," Jessica clarified. "I meant in terms of cuddling by the light of the fire, or kissing underneath the mistletoe. We're still too early in our relationship to hop into the sack."

"And, we both know how apt you are to do that," Karen added.

I shook my head. "Do you have to keep bringing up that incident in Barbados with my former girlfriend, Elaine Abraham?" I protested.

"She dumped you for another man, Gary," Jessica stated, "you are damn right we're going to do so every chance we get."

"And, that was his second offense," Karen noted. "Need I remind you of my hotel room in Calgary during the World Winter

Games security detail we were both a part of?"

"That was 25 years ago," I argued.

"Nevertheless," the specter stated. "You fucked me then, just like you fucked Elaine. The only difference is I didn't leave you for another man."

"I don't want to be lumped into the same category as your previous conquests, Gary," Jessica replied. "I love you, and I don't think sex should be an integral part of our relationship; at least, not yet."

"I love you, too, Jessica," I responded. "I completely understand where you're coming from. There have been times in the past where I have been too quick to jump in the sheets with a woman I cared about. But, like my practices here at work, I'm trying to improve on that."

"And, we commend you for that," my partner noted. "We know it hasn't been easy, and there have been times where things haven't gone as smoothly as you hoped, but at least you're trying."

"Thank you kindly," I said. "But, getting back to the matter at hand: is it alright if Phil tagged along with us during our vacation? I'll ask him if he wants to come, but I wanted to pass it by the two of you first."

Karen and Jessica looked at each other, then back at me.

"Could you give us a second to discuss this further?" Karen asked.

I got up from my chair, and turned towards the Break Room. "Sure thing, ladies," I answered. "I'm going to grab some coffee. Would you like anything, Amerson?"

"I'm fine, Celdom, thanks," she responded.

I headed off to fetch my mug of mud, and allowed the girls a chance to debate my proposal further.

~ * * * ~

"So, what do you think?" Jessica asked the specter. "Should I let Gary drag Phil along with us to the cottage?"

"It's your call," Karen mused. "I know you wanted to use this vacation to spend some quality time with him in a non-work setting, and having Phil there will put a serious crimp in those plans."

Jessica nodded. "That it will, but at the same time, Gary does raise some valid concerns. I care about Phil, too. He's a good friend of Gary's, and I don't want him going back down that road to ruin, I know writers are tortured souls, but you usually think about it happening with alcohol or drugs, not gambling."

"Gambling is still a devastating addiction to have. So, maybe it is good to remove him away from the avenues where he could get his drug here in Toronto.

"Perhaps, but I know there is a slot facility up the road from Gary's cottage. I know Phil doesn't drive, and he'd be stupid to try and con either of us to drive him up there. If Phil's going to gamble, he'll find a way to get there."

"True, but maybe there is a way where you can keep his mind off of gambling, and get some alone time with Gary in the process."

Jessica blinked. "And, how do you suggest we do that?"

Karen thought for a moment. "Well, Gary is bringing Benny to the cottage, too, right? You could get Phil to take the dog out for the odd walk, and that would give you and Gary the alone time you're craving for."

Jessica mulled the possibility. Having Benny tag along would be a perfect foil for Phil, in her opinion. Granted, the walks wouldn't be very far since my cottage was on the shores of Rice Lake in the Kawarthas, and there were only side roads in the area. However, it would still afford Jessica the opportunity to have some alone time with me.

My girlfriend's face lit up. "My God, Karen, you're a genius. I never would have thought about the Benny angle. Okay then, I'll tell Gary that Phil can tag along. I just hope Phil doesn't feel out of place up there."

Karen nodded. "We'll see. It also depends if Phil is up to coming along with us."

~ * * * ~

After Jessica gave me the green light, I called my writing friend up on the phone. As per his usual habit, he picked up on the second ring.

"Hello, Phil?" I introduced. "It's Detective Celdom."

"Oh hey, Detective," he responded. "What's going on?"

I explained to him my offer about spending Christmas up at my cottage with the rest of us. He seemed hesitant at the notion.

"I don't know, Gary. Are you sure I wouldn't be a third wheel? I mean, I'm sure Detective Amerson wants to spend some quality time with you."

"That was her concern, too. However, like me, we were worried about you spending time alone. No one ought to do that during the holidays, so we're wondering if you'd like to join us."

Phil thought about it for a moment. "I guess I could bring my Netbook, and work on something up there. That way, I won't always be in you guys' hair."

I added, "And, Jessica seems to think you could take Benny out for the occasional walk whenever he needs it."

I could almost feel the sarcasm oozing through the receiver. "Ah ha," he recognized. "So, there is a method to her approval. She wants me to be a pro-bono dog walker whenever she wants to be alone with you."

"Now that you mention it, it does seem somewhat convenient; not that anything would happen between her and I. Regardless, the offer is still on the table. So, are you in?"

Silence filled the air, as Phil contemplated the offer on the table. A few moments later, the writer came back with his answer.

"Alright then," he responded. "I'll do it; I'll come along with you guys. Anything would be better than the turkey frozen dinner I would've had anyway at my place."

Phil and I shot the shit for a while longer, discussing the woes of the local pro hockey team. On the whole, Phil sounded appreciative of the invite, even though Jessica had some ulterior motives for his visit. However, at least he wouldn't be alone over the holidays, and that was my prime directive. With the plans set in place, I let the girls know Phil accepted the offer. Jessica was still unimpressed with the added guest in our junket, but she knew it was a noble thing to do.

After my partner-cum-girlfriend calmed down, the two of us finished our paperwork for the day, then headed our respective ways home. We decided to drive up to my cottage on Saturday, and return to Toronto the Friday after, which turned out to be Boxing Day. I was looking forward to the time away from the city. However, as much as I tried to get away, work always had a way of finding me.

CHAPTER 2

Saturday afternoon rolled around, and I had picked up Jessica from her place in Cabbagetown. We were turning off from the Don Valley Parkway onto Highway 401, making our way to Phil's place to pick him up before heading to my cottage on Rice Lake. I was feeling a tad uncomfortable driving the highway; not because of the holiday traffic, but because my girlfriend was still smoldering over the fact I had invited my best friend. In her eyes, this was supposed to be an intimate vacation for her and me. However, at the hour we were traveling, she could have been sporting what some people refer to as 'resting bitch face', for all I knew. Thankfully, there was a coffee shop not far from Phil's apartment, so I was praying some hot caffeine would lighten her tired and sour mood.

"Where are we now?" my partner asked.

"We're just coming up on Warden now," I announced. "We should be at Phil's in about a half hour, or so."

"I'm still not happy he's tagging along with us."

I sighed. "I know, dear, but better he's with people he knows over the holiday than to be stuck alone at home."

Jessica yawned, a sign of the early hour. "I suppose so. It's a shame his aunt is feeling under the weather during this time of year."

"I agree; falling ill during the festive season is never fun. I remember one year, as a kid, I got sick over Christmas. It was the worst one I've ever had."

Jessica asked, "But, the presents made up for it, didn't they?"

I nodded. "They did a little, but the best part about the holidays is spending it with those you care about, and you don't get much of an opportunity to do so when your head is stuck in a bucket beside your bed."

7

My partner gagged at the thought. "Thank you for the mental image."

"Sorry, honey, but that's what happened."

"Be it as it may, can I ask we try to forgo any gruesomeness this vacation?"

"I'm with you on that. We've had our share of murders, shootings, and stabbings at work. That's why I think it's good to get out of the city for the holidays. It will give us a chance to decompress, and enjoy the time away from the craziness."

A noble ambition to have, I thought. Alas, when you're an officer of the law, such hopes can prove to be pipe dreams.

We pulled into the front driveway of Phil's apartment building, and he was already downstairs waiting for us with his knapsack slung over his shoulder, and carrying a duffel bag with the rest of his clothes. I popped open the trunk, and he placed his wares inside before climbing into the back seat with Benny.

"You guys made good time," my friend observed.

"Traffic was relatively light coming from Jessica's place," I stated.

"It'll probably be a different story once we hit the 401," he mused.

"It didn't seem too bad coming across from the DVP," Jessica commented. "But, it might be a different story once we hit Durham Region."

Phil fastened his seat belt, and we were back on our way. "Thanks again for inviting me," he said. "Things were awfully quiet in the apartment without Jim around."

"When did he leave for his relatives' in Vancouver?" I asked.

"A few days ago," Phil replied. "He's staying with his mom and

8

step-dad while out there, but his sister lives out that way, too."

"You didn't tell me Jim had a sister," I commented.

"I didn't think it would come up," my friend stated. "But yeah, Jim has a half-sister; born to his mom and step-dad."

"Is Jim's dad still alive?" Jessica queried.

"He is," Phil said. "Jim Sr. lives down in Parkdale with his girlfriend, and he usually spends Christmas Day with them, but for some reason, Jim's mom and sister were adamant about him flying out there this year."

Jessica blinked. "Is Jim's mom falling ill?" she asked.

Phil laughed. "No," he answered, "she's got a clean bill of health. But, I suspect Jim's half-sister has something in the works. Based on what I've overheard when Jim's talked to his mom, his half-sister, and her boyfriend will probably announce their engagement during the holidays."

"That would be a valid reason, if any, to be in attendance," I mused.

Phil sighed, and I could tell the disheartened tone in his voice. "I suppose so," he said.

Although he wouldn't admit it, I could tell Phil was still upset about being alone. Yes, he had been living with Jim for almost six years, but his heart was still smarting from how his previous relationship had ended. Phil was in an on-again/off-again relationship with a young woman from London, named Amy. Amy was able to make Phil feel love in his heart for someone; an emotion he hadn't experienced since his perceived soul mate: a former girlfriend from Calgary named Amber, passed away fourteen years ago.

There was only one problem: while Phil had much love for Amy, the feelings were not mutual. It was something that tormented my friend emotionally. He would chalk it up to Amy's immaturity; not knowing what she wanted out of a relationship. However, when he learned she had her eye on a local neighbor of hers, Phil washed his hands of Amy completely, and had been enjoying life as a single guy for a year. Yet, the memory of the lass from London still ate away at him.

I attempted to assure my friend. "Don't worry, Phil," I said. "I think spending time out of the city will do us a world of good."

My friend sighed "I hope so, Gary," he replied. "There's nothing worse than being alone for the holidays. That's why I'm thankful you guys invited me up."

I glanced over at my partner, and saw she was still fuming over the added passenger. Jessica sighed, and forced a smile. "Think nothing of it," she noted. "We're glad you could come along."

As much as the three of us didn't want to admit it, the rest of the drive to the Kawarthas was an uncomfortable one at best.

~ * * * ~

In a bid to make sure Phil wouldn't be triggered by my cottage's proximity to the racetrack and slot machine facility on the southern outskirts of Peterborough, I decided to take a back route on my way to the cottage. The course took us through the small town of Millbrook where there was a reasonably-sized grocery store, and other shops. While there was the smaller hamlet of Bewdley closer to my vacation dwelling, the corner store didn't have as vast a selection of grocery items needed for the festive meal I was planning to cook for the four of us. I made mention of this to my traveling companions, so if either of them wanted to pick up anything of note, they knew what the shopping options were. After getting a few bags of groceries, and squeezing them into my trunk with the rest of our luggage, we continued along the side roads to my modest cottage on Rice Lake.

As we pulled down the snow-covered dirt road to my cottage, we noticed some bright lights in the distance. However, these weren't the normal colors of holiday lights one might come to

xect, but those from a patrol car. We drove further down the road, and saw the patrol car was parked in front of the home of my neighbor, Maggie MacPhearson. We pulled into my driveway, and went next door to investigate. I asked Phil to take Benny for a walk while Jessica and I paid Maggie a visit. Phil appreciated the offer, as it gave him a chance to stretch his legs.

We entered the residence, and found Maggie sobbing in her living room, her Christmas tree laid bare, and one of the two officers was questioning her.

"Maggie," I interrupted, "what happened?"

"Excuse me, sir," one of the Constables queried. "But, who are you?"

I identified myself. "Detective Gary Celdom, Toronto P.D. I own the cottage next door to Miss MacPhearson's. This is my partner, Detective Jessica Amerson."

The Constable identified himself. "My apologies, Detectives. I'm Constable Jenner of the Ontario Provincial Police -- Bewdley Detachment, and this is my partner, Constable Kassian."

"We didn't mean to intrude, Constable," Jessica explained. "We just came up from Toronto, and saw the lights of your patrol car. Is everything alright?"

Maggie broke through her sobs. "Not really," she said. "My home was broken into, and all of my Christmas presents were stolen."

11

CHAPTER 3

Constables Jenner and Kassian interviewed the three of us to get
our sides of the story; although, there wasn't much information
they could get from Jessica and myself. After the interview, the
Constables gave us their cards, and left the scene. When things
had settled down for a bit, I helped fix some coffee for us. I
returned with the steaming mugs, and took a seat with the ladies
in Maggie's living room. My seasonal neighbor was still shaken
up from the events.

"So, whoever did this cleaned you out?" Jessica asked.

"Yes, Detective Amerson," Maggie replied.

"Please, call me 'Jessica'," my partner insisted.

"Sorry, Jessica," Maggie apologized. "I was running some
errands in town, and came home to find everything underneath
my tree was stolen."

I began to worry. "They didn't take Biscuit, too, did they?" I
queried.

Maggie shook her head. "No, thank goodness," she said. "The
errand was actually a vet visit for her. She has a clean bill of
health, but right now, I'm a nervous wreck."

I nodded. "Understandably so," I noted.

Jessica leaned towards me, and whispered, "Who is Biscuit?"

I whispered back, "Maggie's 2-year old Pomeranian."

After I explained Maggie's animal companion to Jessica, Biscuit
came toddling in from Maggie's bedroom, yipping all the way. I
presumed Maggie kept her penned up in there while she was
being interviewed by the Constables, so as not to disrupt the
interview. Upon seeing Biscuit, my partner fell in love with the
adorable pup.

"Oh," Jessica cooed, "she is a cutie."

Maggie nodded. "Yes," she added. "She's been my pride and joy ever since I got her."

"I can see why you would be upset if the thief, or thieves, took her," my partner mused. "Did you get her from the Humane Society?"

"If I may interject here," I said. "Maggie volunteers for a dog rescue shelter out in Manitoba."

"It's true," my neighbor affirmed. "All of the dogs I have owned were one-time residents at the shelter."

"That's quite a noble cause you support," Jessica observed.

"It is," Maggie replied. "I also help out by creating various promotional materials for them. So, they're appreciative of my work."

The three of us continued to chat for a while, then there was a knock upon Maggie's door. I was asked to get up to answer it because Maggie was still antsy about the earlier events, and Biscuit was yipping at whomever was standing outside. When I opened the door, my writing friend stood before me.

"Hi, Phil," I greeted.

"Hey, Gary," he reported. "I finished walking Benny, and he's resting back at your cottage. Is everything alright in here?"

"Who is it, Gary?" Maggie asked.

"It's my friend who came up with us for the holiday," I informed.

"Well, don't just let him stand out in the cold," my neighbor requested. "Tell him to come on in for a spell."

I ushered Phil into Maggie's abode, and he appreciated the invite.

"It's a nippy evening out there," he said, "But, such as the case when you're walking a pet by a lake in Cottage County."

"You own a dog, too?" Maggie asked.

Jessica clarified, "No, he was walking Gary's husky for him while we were over here."

I recognized the two had not been introduced. "Oh, how rude of me," I apologized. "Maggie MacPhearson, this is Phil Bennett."

"Tis a pleasure to meet you, Maggie," Phil said, extending his hand.

Maggie smiled, and shook my friend's hand. "Likewise, I'm sure," she replied.

Biscuit stopped yipping when Phil introduced himself. The writer offered his hand to the Pomeranian, and after sniffing it, Biscuit began to lick it.

"I guess she accepts you," I observed.

"Really?" Phil doubted. "I thought she might be intimidated by my size."

Maggie smiled. "Nope," she said. "She likes you."

"She is quite adorable, I do admit," the writer smiled back before breaking into a cooing voice while petting Biscuit. "Who's a pretty girl?"

Jessica noticed there was a faint sparkle in Maggie's eye when she met Phil. My partner looked at me with a raised eyebrow. Me, being a typical male, didn't pick up on it; then again, neither did Phil.

"I hate to end our visit," I said. "But, I better head back to my cottage and feed Benny. He must be starving by now."

"Are you sure you're going to be alright here, Maggie?" my

partner asked.

Maggie nodded. "I'll be fine, thanks," she replied.

Jessica reached into her purse, and handed Maggie one of her business cards. "If you need anything," she said, "feel free to give me, or Gary, a call."

"Or, you can just pop over anytime, if we're in," I clarified.

Maggie began to relax. "Thanks, you guys," she appreciated. "Knowing you're nearby will make me rest easier."

"Nice meeting you, Maggie," Phil commented.

The three of us left the abode, and Maggie beamed a smile. She said to herself, "I think you'll be seeing me again later this week, Phil Bennett."

~ * * * ~

When we returned to my cottage, Benny was there to greet us. I made my way to the kitchen to fetch my husky his dinner. Phil moved his luggage into his room, and Jessica took a seat on my living room couch. Once Benny was fed, I started preparing dinner for myself and my boarders for the next few days.

Jessica called out to me, "Maggie seems like a nice woman."

"She is," I replied. "She's been living next door to me for a few years now. She doesn't poke her head out much; just goes to work, then stays in her place for most of the time."

"The poor thing," my partner commented. "She seems like she needs some companionship."

"What do you mean?" I asked. "Maggie has Biscuit to keep her company."

Jessica got up and walked towards the kitchen. "You know what I mean, Gary," she said. "I think she might benefit more with some human interaction."

"Now, Jessica," I cautioned. "I'm happy with the woman I'm with now. You're not going to pawn me off on my neighbor."

Jessica rolled her eyes, as she stood in the doorway. "I don't mean you, you bonehead. I'm talking about Phil."

A familiar ghostly apparition appeared, and sat at the kitchen table. "You noticed it, too, Jessica?" Karen asked.

My partner nodded. "I certainly did," she affirmed.

I was confused. "What the hell are you two talking about?" I asked.

"Oh, come on, Gary," Karen said, "You didn't notice how Maggie was looking at Phil when he was petting Biscuit? She saw something in him that she liked."

I turned to my girlfriend. "Was that why you shot me that look over at her place?" I quizzed.

"Well, duh!" Jessica quipped. "It was that look of... well, I don't think I would call it 'love at first sight', but it was definitely a 'like'."

I tried to wrap my head around what the women were saying. "Hold on, now," I stammered. "Are you saying that Maggie is smitten with Phil?"

"I don't think it has developed that far yet," Karen corrected. "But, I do think she is harboring an interest in him."

Phil returned from his room to investigate what was going on. "You two having a chat with Gary's former fiancée?"

While Phil knew of Karen's existence, he still could not see or hear her. She had only revealed herself to myself and Jessica, with the latter occurring during the hostage situation where I was reunited with Phil three years before. It was during that case,

Karen advised my partner to commence a personal relationship with me, and we had been involved ever since.

"We kind of were," I confirmed.

"Was it about the situation at Maggie's?" he asked.

I nodded. "It was," I replied.

We filled Phil in on what had happened, and how it appeared Maggie and Biscuit would be spending Christmas without any gifts to give to their loved ones. The notion brought a bit of sadness to the writer. Like myself, he believed no one should spend the holidays without anything to give. It was something he regretfully experienced himself.

He told Jessica and me a story of when he was in the grips of his illness. Phil had gambled away all of the money he had set aside for presents for his family. It was an act which made him realize he needed help, so he sought counseling for his addiction. He has had his ups and downs since then; the most notable was his relapse when Jessica and I picked him up after he was ejected from the off-track horse betting facility in the Beaches. The relapse occurred six months after the Christmas present gambling binge. Phil had been clean since, but like any addict the illness never goes away completely. That was why we brought him up here, in hopes we could curtail any urges he might have had by being alone at home.

"I wish there was something we could do to help her out," I said.

"I know this would be wrong for me to suggest this because I know you two are on vacation," Phil remarked.

"Oh, no," Jessica interrupted. "No, no, no. I'm not going to spend my time off working on a case."

"I'm not saying you'd have to do it directly," the writer explained. "I know the Bewdley Detachment of the O.P.P. have dibs on the case, and they might be sensitive about their toes being stepped on. However, if you could assist in the investigation..."

"Absolutely not!" Jessica objected. "I didn't come all the way here to work during the holidays. If I wanted to do that, I would've stayed at home, and I'm sure Gary agrees with me, right?"

I thought about it for a second. "Well...," I started.

"Oh, God," Jessica cringed. "You're seriously considering this, aren't you?"

"Not entirely," I stumbled. "Yes, Maggie is my friend and neighbor, and she does need help in retrieving her stolen gifts if they can even be recovered at all. However, we both agreed to come up here in a bid to get away from the beat. If we spent the few days we have away from the Division to work on a case the local authorities might not allow us to assist in, it would seem moot."

Phil shook his head in disbelief. "You know," he stated, "Peter Grossman's character would've leapt at Maggie's case; much to the chagrin of Cal Kenneth Robbins' character."

I shot a look at my friend. "Look, Phil," I accused. "I know you're a fan of <u>Northern Winds,</u> but that's a television series; this is a real life case here. As much as Maggie is my neighbor and friend, I'm not willing to stick my neck out for her like a fictional federal police officer."

Phil turned away in a huff, and proceeded to walk out of the kitchen. He stopped at the doorway, turned to me, and said, "You know, Gary, I thought you were an honorable detective; willing to help out the common civilian. But now, all I see is just another union employee who is only in it for himself. I'll be in my room." Phil marched down the hallway, with Benny following him, and slammed his bedroom door shut.

So far, my plans for a quiet week away with those I cared about had gotten off to a rocky start.

CHAPTER 4

Jessica and I sat in the living room of my cottage, and we were both furious. Phil had accused both of us of 'being a couple of union employees who were only looking out for ourselves.' After everything we had done to make him feel welcome up here, he went and pointed a judgmental finger at my partner and me just because we weren't willing to help track down the person -- or persons -- responsible for breaking into Maggie's place, stealing her Christmas gifts in the process. While Karen was quick to point out Phil had only accused me of being a unionized toady, Jessica took umbrage to the writer's accusations; implying she had the same beliefs.

"I'm as upset as you are, Jessica," I said. "For him to insinuate we're not willing to do our duty because we're on holiday is uncalled for."

The specter got up from her seat. "To be honest," Karen noted, "you're not willing to do your duty."

Jessica and I blinked. "Excuse me?" I asked.

"Think about it, you two," my former fiancée explained. "An officer's credence is 'to serve and protect'. Maggie needs help in finding out who stole her Christmas away from her. Now, I have no doubt the Bewdley Detachment O.P.P. can do their job; however, if they can get some additional assistance by a couple of out-of-town detectives who happen to be in the area, that might expedite the capture of the thief, or thieves, and the recovery of the missing wares."

Jessica and I looked at each other, and we both nodded in agreement. Karen was right in her accusation; we weren't doing our civil duty. After some further contemplation, we decided to visit the O.P.P. detachment in Bewdley in the morning to offer our assistance on the case. There was no guarantee it would be accepted, but it was the least we could do. However, there was one person we needed to inform of our decision, and Jessica and I hoped we could iron things out with him from earlier.

I knocked on Phil's door. "Phil," I requested, "could we talk for a moment?"

"It's your cottage," he spat. "Do whatever the hell you want."

I opened the door, and both Jessica and I entered.

After a pregnant pause, the writer continued to fume. "Well, you two wanted to say something?"

"Look, Phil," Jessica started. "We know you were upset about our initial decision not to help out on the investigation over at Maggie's place, but Gary and I talked it over, and we've decided to offer our assistance."

Phil still doubted us. "This isn't some lip service the two of you are giving me, is it?" he asked.

"Nope," I confirmed. "Karen talked to us about it, and she pointed out we were being selfish in our original assessment. We weren't living up to our duty, so after some discussion, we decided to lend a hand in the investigation, if the guys in Bewdley allow us to. We'll be going out there in the morning to hopefully discuss the case."

Phil hung his head and sighed. "I guess I should apologize for what I said," he commented.

"It wouldn't hurt," I suggested. I felt a ghostly smack upside the back of my head after speaking those words. "Sorry," I continued, "that came out wrong."

"No, no," Phil corrected. "I deserve that. I don't blame you two for being upset with me. I said what I did out of spite, and for that, I apologize. It's just that with Maggie being your neighbor, I thought you would've leapt at the chance to help her out; just like you've helped me in the past."

"Phil, buddy," I stated, "I've had to clean up my act quite a bit over the recent months at work. You don't know how much I've crossed the line by not following proper protocol."

Jessica nodded. "It's true," she added. "It's a surprise our supervisors have allowed Gary to stay on for as long as he has. I'm sure Lt. Davies has a hand in keeping him on, but Gary is still a work in progress."

Phil chuckled. "Kind of like me, to a degree," he mused. "Me with my gambling, and Gary with him following procedure."

"I guess you could argue that," I replied. "But, be it as it may, we realized the error in our thinking, and I just hope we can spend the rest of the holiday without any further animosity between the three of us."

The writer nodded. "I'd like that," he said. "Now, what about dinner? I'm famished."

I laughed, and Jessica rolled her eyes with a chuckle. The three of us made our way back to the kitchen, and I prepared a reasonable meal for the three of us. We didn't let on about Maggie's possible infatuation with Phil; figuring he would find out by himself in due time. However, if it takes him as long as it did about me finding about Jessica's interest in her partner, Phil might not clue in until we were ready to return to Toronto.

CHAPTER 5

The next day, Jessica and I made our way to the O.P.P. detachment in Bewdley. Once there, we met with the commanding officer, Sgt. Betchel. As I had first thought, he didn't seem too enthused with the idea of two out-of-town detectives assisting with the case. However, after we explained to him we would do our best not to step on the toes of Constables Jenner and Kassian during the investigation, Sgt. Betchel accepted our offer, albeit reluctantly.

He led us to the desks of the two Constables, and like their superior at first, they were not too pleased with our presence.

"With all due respect, Sargent," Jenner complained. "We're both highly capable Constables who can handle this case on our own."

"I understand your concern," Sgt. Betchel stated. "However, on a case like this, it doesn't hurt to have a couple extra sets of legs."

"We've assured Sgt. Betchel we wouldn't impede your ongoing investigation," I reported.

"We will assist both of you in any way possible," Jessica added. "All we ask is that you give both Detective Celdom and myself a chance."

Constables Kassian and Jenner looked at each other. They were both still reluctant to accept our help, but when their superior officer handed down the edict, there was not much choice they had in the matter.

Kassian sighed. "Fine," he fumed," you can help us out. But remember, we do things a little differently out here than you guys do in Toronto."

"We understand that," Jessica said. "We all have a common goal here: find whomever is responsible for the break-in of the MacPhearson estate, and if possible, salvaging whatever gifts were stolen from her."

"Finding the criminal would be easier than finding the missing gifts," Jenner mused. "But, we will do our best."

Sgt. Betchel said, "I'll leave you four alone. I suspect the Constables will want to fill the Detectives in on their findings, so far."

"Thank you kindly, Sargent," I replied.

The Sargent returned to his office. Once he was gone, both Jessica and I noticed there was still hesitation from Kassian and Jenner. The two Constables didn't like two Detectives from Toronto horning in on their turf. It was akin to members from a higher ranking police force taking over the interrogation of a suspect because their investigation superseded the existing one from the lower-tiered jurisdiction. The office difference was, the O.P.P. was the level above Jessica and me. From an optic standpoint, the two of us were seen as usurping the work of Jenner and Kassian, which was not our intention at all. We only wanted to get Maggie's stuff back. Regardless, Jenner and Kassian had no other choice but to follow Sgt. Betchel's orders, much to their chagrin.

~ * * * ~

While Jessica and I were busy working out in Bewdley, Phil kept himself occupied at my cottage, typing away on his latest manuscript. Benny was laying on the floor beside his chair, keeping the writer company. He was struggling with a scene, and had gotten up to make himself a cup of tea when he heard a knock at the door. He took the kettle off the stove burner, so it wouldn't boil dry, and went to see who was visiting. When he noticed it was Maggie, he opened the door, and invited her in.

"Gary isn't here," he informed.

"That's okay," Maggie said. "My place was feeling empty without my gifts, and I noticed you were over here, so I decided to stop by and say 'Hello.'"

"I bet you're still shaken up from the robbery."

Maggie nodded. "I am. You never expect to be broken into, let alone during this time of year."

"Thieves usually strike at the most opportune moment, and a home with a plethora of presents underneath the tree would be a residence that's ripe for the picking."

Maggie looked at Phil, and a smile formed upon her face. Phil looked back at her inquisitively. He queried, "Why are you looking at me like that?"

"I'm impressed with your vocabulary. Not many people would know how to use the word 'plethora' in the proper context."

Phil chuckled. "It's something I have been working on over the years, given my current profession."

Maggie was curious. "And, may I inquire as to what Phil Bennett does for a living?"

"Right now, I'm a writer, an 'author-in-training', if you will."

Maggie blinked. "Really? Have you ever had anything published before?"

Phil shook his head, "Unfortunately, not yet. I have a few works in various stages of editing and completion, but I'm kind of worried that my work wouldn't be good enough to win over a publisher."

My neighbor thought for a moment. "Maybe I could help you out?"

"Oh? Do you know of a publisher who would be interested in looking at my work?"

Maggie laughed. "I don't mean with that. I proofread thesis submissions for the School of Liberal Arts at Trent University. What I can do is go over your manuscripts for you. You know, checking the grammar and sentence structure."

"That would be wonderful, if you could. However, I don't have much at the moment to pay you. You know, social assistance recipient, and all."

Maggie smiled, and patted Phil's hand. "Don't worry about it. I'm willing to offer my 'editing services' pro-bono."

Phil was touched by Maggie's gesture. Here was a woman who had her Christmas stolen from her, but was willing to help out a man she had just met at his craft. It was a sign that the spirit of the season was alive and well out in Cottage Country. Phil struggled to think of what he could do to repay my neighbor. Maggie was insistent Phil ought not to worry about it, but he still wanted to do something to make it up to her. Only, he didn't know what it would be at the current juncture. However, for a temporary placebo, he came up with a solution.

"I was in the process of making tea when you came by," Phil explained. "Would you like a cup?"

Maggie smiled at Phil. "I would love one," she replied.

~ * * * ~

Jessica and I went over the case notes Kassian and Jenner had amassed since the beginning of the investigation. We rubbed our foreheads, trying to determine if there was a pattern with any of the other break-and-enters that had happened in the area. It appeared whomever was responsible for them had hit a number of homes in the previous few weeks. I excused myself for a moment to hit the restroom to relieve myself after a liquid diet of coffee for the past few hours. Upon arriving, I was visited by a familiar specter.

Karen mused, "This case is proving more difficult than you thought, huh?"

I almost sprayed the wall when I jumped at the sound of the voice of my dead fiancée. "Jesus, Karen," I accused. "You need to work on your appearance times."

25

The specter rolled her eyes. "Oh, come on, Gary. It's not like I haven't seen it before."

"And, to what do I owe this latest appearance?"

"I was just pointing out that you and Jessica seem to be struggling with finding a lead on this case."

I nodded. "We are; there's just so many notes Kassian and Jenner have gathered on the case. It's a lot of information to digest."

"Can I ask you something?"

I finished emptying my bladder, and moved over to the sink to wash my hands. "What is it?"

Karen leaned against the wall beside me. "In all of the notes those two have compiled, did they happen to include a composite sketch of the suspect?"

I thought for a moment, and the revelation dawned on me. There wasn't a sketch of the suspect in their files. Karen had stumbled upon something that was missing which would help the four of us a great deal.

I finished drying my hands. "Karen, you're a genius. Surely, someone should have seen him, or at least have some surveillance video footage of him."

"You would think, 'and please, don't call me 'Shirley.'""

I chuckled at the pop culture reference, and thanked my former fiancée for her advice. I left the restroom, and went on a hunt for the two Constables. I found Kassian on the phone, taking a call. He saw me approach, and told me to hold on for a second. I was a little perturbed about being put off momentarily, but when he finished his call, I learned it was for good reason.

"Celdom," he informed, "go fetch Amerson. The four of us are going to check out a department store in Peterborough."

"A robbery up there?" I asked.

"We have a report of a tractor trailer being stolen from a loading dock. We're going to attempt to obtain the surveillance tapes to see if it's the same guy responsible for the other thefts in the area."

I blinked. "A tractor trailer? He's going for the big haul now."

I made my way to Jessica's temporary desk, while Kassian rounded up Jenner. We hoped this would provide the break in the case we were looking for. Little did we realize this was merely the tip of the iceberg.

CHAPTER 6

The four of us arrived at the department store on the outskirts of Peterborough. After identifying ourselves, we made our way to the Security Office to see if there was any footage from the loading dock heist. We were fortunate enough to learn they still had the footage of the robbery. After seeing what we were looking for, we requested a copy of the digital media, and admonished the workers on the loading dock for leaving a shipment of merchandise unattended during this time of year.

They apologized for their negligence to their supervisors; however, we told the store manager to go easy on them, as they didn't know there was someone we were on the lookout for. We informed the manager we would do our best to recoup the stolen merchandise, and have it back on their shelves in time for the Boxing Day sales. I knew it seemed like a hollow promise for us to make, but for the thief to have done such a brazen crime during the festive season, it made us more vigilant to find whomever was responsible.

~ * * * ~

Back in her home, Maggie MacPhearson sat on her couch with her Pomeranian, Biscuit. She was in the process of brushing the canine. It was a sensation the little girl enjoyed, far more than getting her toenails clipped. However, this was part of the grooming rituals Maggie made her pet endure, as it was a way to save money in the long run. While Maggie and Biscuit lived humbly in their abode, my neighbor was still upset over the fact someone had broken into their home, and stole the presents from underneath her tree. Maggie looked at the barren space where the wrapped wares once sat, and she emitted a disheartened sigh.

After a few moments of wallowing in her misery, someone knocked upon Maggie's door. Considering what had transpired a couple nights before, she got up off her couch, grabbed a baseball bat, and cautiously made her way to the entrance. Maggie peered through the knothole, and saw my guest standing outside. Upon recognizing Phil's presence, she tucked the bat in the corner, attempted to brush off the excess dog hair that clung to her clothes, and opened the door.

"Well," she beamed, "if it isn't Phil Bennett."

"Good afternoon, Maggie," he said. "Do you mind if I come in?"

The homeowner invited the writer inside. "Oh yes, please do."

Phil shunned his coat and boots. "Thank you kindly."

"And, to what do I owe this visit from the budding writer?"

Phil chuckled. "Well, I was taking a break from writing, and I thought to myself, 'You know, Maggie is next door all alone, and she's probably still shaken up from what happened. I should go over, and check to see how she's doing.'"

"That was very thoughtful of you, Phil. You're right, I'm still pretty upset about having Christmas stolen away from me. I'm the type of person who loves the season, but after this happened, I'm beginning to lose my passion for it."

Phil nodded. "I can understand that. Christmas is supposed to be a time for sharing the joy and merriment of the holidays. To have some -- if you'll excuse my language -- greedy asshole steal it away from not only yourself, but other families, as well, it can be quite disheartening."

Maggie sighed. "It is. I just hope Gary and Jessica can help find whomever is responsible for these heinous acts."

"Gary and Jessica are both good detectives. I'm sure with the collaboration with the Bewdley O.P.P., they will get to the bottom of this case."

Maggie invited Phil to take a seat. "I'm going to fix myself some coffee. Would you like some?"

"I would love a cup, please." The writer sat down upon the couch beside Biscuit, and proceeded to rub her fur. "I find coffee helps fuel my muse in the creative process."

Maggie excused herself, and headed into her kitchen. She called back out to her visitor, "You mentioned you're an 'author-in-training'. If you don't mind me asking, what genre do you write?"

"Right now, I write mystery stories. However, if you were to look on my social media account, most of my friends appear to be romance or fantasy authors."

Maggie seemed hesitant. "Now, when you say 'fantasy', you don't mean like erotic stuff, right?"

Phil laughed. "Oh, no, no. I mean, like, knights, dragons, elves... that kind of genre."

Maggie returned from the kitchen with two steaming mugs of java. She set one of them on the coffee table in front of Phil. "I didn't know how you take it, so I made it the same way I do: one teaspoon of sugar and two shots of milk."

Phil appreciated the gesture. "This will be fine, thank you."

Maggie set her mug down upon the table, and moved Biscuit to the opposite side of her, so she could sit closer to the writer. Phil sipped on his beverage, while Maggie resumed her questioning. "So, you write mystery stories, and your best friend is a detective. How does Gary feel about you writing such a genre?"

"Surprisingly, he's supportive of it. In fact, I actually picked his brain for one of them."

Phil recounted the story where he interviewed me for research. I told him about an old case where I had traveled to Barbados to investigate the murder of my former partner, Rob McManus. It was during this case where I met my former girlfriend, Elaine Abraham, a waitress in a seedy bar. It was a relationship that did not please Karen, and when she learned of the whole story, Jessica. However, it was through Elaine where I learned about the writing challenge, NoMo. Thanks to my first attempt in participating in it, it led me into meeting Phil, and helped form the friendship he and I established to this day.

"That's fascinating," Maggie commented. "I would've thought he wouldn't be supportive of such an endeavor."

"One would think that," Phil mused. "But, he's been a good friend and confidant for the past few years."

"I think it's amazing the two of you were able to reconnect at a fan convention a year later. Might I ask what sort of convention it was?"

"You're going to laugh at this, but it was for one of our favorite television series, Northern Winds."

Maggie's eyes lit up. "Oh, my God, I love that show! I am so into Peter Grossman, it's not even funny."

Phil blinked. "Really, you're a Peter Grossman fan?"

Maggie nodded. "Yes, I saw his World War I movie, and absolutely loved his acting. Later, I went on the Internet, and looked to see what other projects he's been involved with. When I saw he was in Northern Winds, I bought the DVD boxed sets, watched the episodes, and fell in love with the quirkiness of the series."

Phil smiled. "Well then, I think you're going to love what I brought over."

Maggie looked puzzled. "What did you bring me?"

Phil reached into his pocket, and pulled out a USB Flash drive. "If you could point me in the direction of your computer, I'll show you."

Maggie told Phil where she kept her desktop, and he excused himself for a few moments. Upon finding the device, he plugged the drive into a free slot, and after maneuvering the mouse, he transferred a file over to Maggie's computer. "It's not much," he stated. "But, I figured it is a little something to help make the season a little merrier for you."

"I'm eager to find out what it is."

"You will, just give it a listen." Phil clicked the mouse a couple more times, and activated the file. A couple of seconds later, the sound of a country guitar filled the air. The melody was rather upbeat while Maggie listened along, but she was shocked when she immediately recognized the person singing.

"Oh, my God," Maggie exclaimed, "that's Peter Grossman singing!"

Phil nodded. "Yes, remember that Season 4 Christmas episode in Northern Winds where Derek McStevens' character sang a little ditty while wearing a cowboy hat adorned with Christmas lights? Well, Peter Grossman expanded on it, and turned it into a full-length holiday song."

"How were you able to get a copy of the song?"

"It was on a charity CD I had bought about a decade or so ago. It turned into my favorite Christmas song, and I wanted to share it with you. The fact you're a Peter Grossman fan, as well, made it even more appropriate."

A wide smile emerged on Maggie's face. "This is a wonderful early Christmas gift, Phil. Thank you ever so much for it."

The writer shrugged it off. "Don't worry about it."

"No, I insist. Is there any way I could repay you for this?"

Phil thought for a moment, then an idea stuck in his brain.

"Could you drive me into Peterborough, please?" he asked. "I want to pick up a few things from the stores there."

~ * * * ~

We arrived back at the detachment in Bewdley, and sought a computer to further analyze the footage we had obtained. We plugged the media into a desktop, and commenced playing and replaying what the surveillance cameras had caught. From what we could tell in the distance, the thief wore a black toque and balaclava to cover his face, as he approached the truck. However, Jessica noticed something in the footage.

"Stop it right there," she requested. "Now, zoom in on the cab of the truck."

Jenner hit a few buttons on the keyboard, and although it was grainy, we were able to grab a screen shot of the thief's face, who had pulled down his balaclava just before he drove away. Jenner attempted to clean up the image, and in a few seconds, we were able to have a reasonable photo to analyze. Kassian took a printout of the screen capture, and started going through the detachment's database of all the wanted suspects in the area. After a few minutes, he was able to match the photo with the suspect.

"What have you got?" I asked.

"His name is Warren Dryden," Kassian reported. "He's got a place by the Pigeon River in South Monaghan."

"Any type of rap sheet on him?" Jessica queried.

"Where do you want me to start?" Kassian said. "He's had previous charges levied against him for possession of a controlled substance."

"Oh, great," I smirked. "We're dealing with a pothead who has resorted to breaking-and-entering to help finance his fixes."

Jenner nodded. "Yes, but there is something else to be concerned about here," he warned. "We're dealing with someone who has broken into homes, and has just shoplifted an entire tractor trailer of merchandise. What's not to say he might have some sort of firearm on his person, in the event he encounters any resistance?"

Jessica and I looked at each other. This was one factor we didn't take into account. Yes, we were dealing with a drug addict or dealer who had gotten into thievery to bankroll his fix, but how was he unloading the stolen merchandise? Was he selling them on the black market, or was he offering it was some sort of weird barter for his stash? What's more, since Dryden was in the narcotic industry, there was a high probability he would want to protect his investment. In doing so, he would likely be in possession of some sort of firearm to assist in his illegal trades. We had to make our next move carefully because one misstep, and any of us would wind up injured or dead. And, winding up at Peterborough Regional Hospital for the holidays was one thing I was hoping to avoid.

CHAPTER 7

"Organizing such a raid is a risky proposition," Jenner stated.

Kassian asked, "Don't you think we should ask Sgt. Betchel for his opinion?"

I had suggested the four of us head up to Dryden's estate to investigate, but it was a huge gamble we would be undertaking. The possibility of there being a confrontation between ourselves and Dryden was more than likely; one which could result in a shootout between us and the suspect. While Jessica and I had been in our share of armed standoffs; it was a scenario foreign to the young Constables.

"What do you think, Amerson," Jenner posed. "Should we talk to our superior beforehand?"

"I know Detective Celdom's proposal is unorthodox for you guys," she commented. "But, if we have a chance to search his premises to find out if he's storing any of the contraband, we could have something substantial we could nail Dryden on."

Jenner was still concerned "I'm not sure about this," he worried. "You two may have a different way of doing things in Toronto, but I'm a little leery about going up there with such a small faction. Are you certain the four of us could handle this on our own?"

"It may seem out of the ordinary for you guys, I admit," I explained. "However, I believe if we can obtain some hard evidence on Dryden, we can put a warrant out for his arrest."

Kassian queried, "And, if Dryden happens to be there, and starts firing a few rounds at us?"

"That's a chance we'll have to take," I replied. "Look, I know you two are still relatively new to your careers, but if you guys can take down Dryden, it'd be a feather in your caps. Just think of how it'll look on your resumes."

The two Constables looked at each other. While I wasn't sure how well my pitch would work, I could tell they were mulling it over. The idea of taking down a criminal like Dryden would be a boon for their careers; however, with such a reward there was also a high risk. Would we run into Dryden when we invaded his property? And, if so, would shots be exchanged? These were things Kassian and Jenner weighed in their minds. Jessica and I could tell they were still having trepidations about the whole situation.

Frustrated, I threw my hands up. "Fine," I sighed, "we'll get Sgt. Betchel's thoughts on the matter."

Kassian breathed a little easier. "We appreciate it, Celdom," he said.

Jenner added, "No hard feelings, but we feel more comfortable getting feedback from our superior."

The two Constables began to make their way to Sgt. Betchel's office. When I felt they were out of earshot, I turned to my partner and muttered, "Talk about being a couple of pussies. They'd never make it in a big city."

"You can't fault them for being hesitant, Gary," Jessica defended. "They probably haven't been involved with such a take down before. Things go at a different pace up here."

"Be it as it may, with a criminal like Dryden at large, you can't go at the investigation half-assed. You're either all-in, or you fold."

My partner chortled. "It's a good thing Phil isn't here. With you using terminology like that, you might have ended up triggering him."

"Hopefully, he's staying out of trouble at my cottage."

"I think he is, but if Maggie's stalking him..."

"She couldn't have developed such an admiration for him that

36

soon, could she?"

Jessica smirked. "You'd be surprised how quickly human infatuation can formulate. Now, come on. Kassian and Jenner are waiting for us in Sgt. Betchel's office."

I begrudgingly got up from my desk, and along with my partner, joined the two Constables in the meeting with their superior officer.

~ * * * ~

Sgt. Betchel wiped his brow. "Let me get this straight," he asked. "The four of you want to head up to Warren Dryden's property, and conduct a search of his premises to see if he's housing any of the stolen merchandise he's accumulated during this crime wave? The same Warren Dryden who has a rap sheet filled with drug and weapon possession offenses?"

"We admit it is a gamble, sir," I replied. "That's why we came to you. Detective Amerson and I were all ready to get the warrant, and head up there..."

Jenner interrupted, "However, Constable Kassian and I thought we should get your advice first. We know it's a risky venture, but the detectives from Toronto appear to be all gung-ho in storming Dryden's property."

"We need to bring him in before he offends again," I defended.

"He is only a suspect on our radar," Kassian countered.

"A suspect?!?" I queried. "We saw him on the security footage stealing a tractor trailer for the department store in Peterborough. You're telling me that's not enough proof for you?"

"Please, everyone," the Sargent pleaded. "You're all giving me a headache here. Detective Amerson, you're the only one who hasn't said anything yet. What's your opinion on this proposal?"

"I'll be the first to admit it this proposed operation will be a risky venture, Sargent," Jessica explained. "However, my partner and I feel the sooner we can get Dryden behind bars, the faster this holiday season can be salvaged for the families affected by Dryden's rampage."

"While we understand the intentions of this mission by our Toronto counterparts," Kassian protested, "both Constable Jenner and myself can't help but stress the likelihood of a possible standoff between the four of us and Dryden at his residence."

Jenner added, "The fact he also has a possible cache of firearms in his possession is something of concern for us, as well. Constable Kassian and I feel this is more than a four-person operation."

Sgt. Betchel rubbed his eyes, and attempted to ease the migraine everyone was giving him. "Okay," he suggested. "I know everyone is up in arms about this whole proposal. However, that being said, since this is Sunday, the earliest we could obtain a warrant for Dryden's arrest is tomorrow morning. So, why don't we all go home, get some rest, and we'll start fresh in the morning. Does that sound fair?"

"But, Sargent," I objected. "If we waited until tomorrow, Dryden could have flown the coop. Isn't there any way we could get the warrant sooner than then?"

"That might be more convenient in Toronto," Sgt. Betchel explained. "But, here in Peterborough County, we are not as 'easily accessed' when it comes to our Justices of the Peace. I know it sounds like a gamble, but I think after the heist Dryden committed earlier today, he might choose to lay low for a while. Besides, there is a good chance he will be mulling around his property tonight. I don't want you four getting into any danger this evening; just go home, rest up, and we'll get at it first thing in the morn."

"We understand, Sargent," Jessica replied. "Come on, Celdom, let's clock out for the day."

I was not impressed with the Sargent's decision; however, there was not much choice I had in the matter. Jessica and I made our way out to the parking lot for the drive back to the cottage. I knew the Sargent's heart was in the right place, but it killed me I would have to wait until the morning to continue with the case. The only problem was, as always, the waiting was the hardest part.

CHAPTER 8

Phil returned to my cottage with Maggie in tow. They were carrying an array of grocery bags into the house. "Thanks for driving me to the grocery stores in Peterborough," he said. "With Gary and Jessica busy with the case, there's no way I could have gotten all the ingredients."

"My pleasure, Phil," she replied. "Although, I'm not sure what you are planning on using all of this for."

"I figured the two of them would be tired and famished after their long day of investigating. So, I decided to fix my famous chili for them both."

"Sounds divine. However, I don't get why you were insistent on finding an Asian grocery store. You know we only have one in the entire Kawarthas."

"Yeah, sorry about that. But, it was the only place I thought would carry the special chili peppers I use in my culinary creation."

Phil unloaded the groceries from the plastic bags. Among them was a small Styrofoam tray, containing a pile of small red Thai Bird's Eye chili peppers, wrapped in cellophane.

"I hope you're not planning on using all of those," Maggie worried.

Phil laughed. "Not really; I only use a specific number for my chili recipe. Too many would send your taste buds into the E.R."

"They can't be that hot, can they?"

"Trust me, they're extremely potent."

Maggie scoffed. "I'll be the judge of that." She peeled back the cellophane, took one of the small peppers from the tray, and began to eat it. After a few seconds, Maggie's eyes grew large, and started gasping for air. "Water," she begged. "Get me some water!"

Phil grabbed a glass from the cupboard, rushed to the refrigerator, and poured my neighbor a tall glass of milk. Maggie grabbed the glass from him, and gulped back the beverage in record time.

"I tried to warn you," Phil scolded.

Maggie attempted to catch her breath. "Holy shit, Phil, you weren't kidding. But, why did you grab some milk instead of water?"

"One thing I've learned over the years of eating spicy foods is they tend to be repelled better with milk or bread. Water would only quench the thirst, but not take away the burning sensation."

Maggie coughed, as the after burn was beginning to subside. "Good thing to know for future reference. So, what goes into Phil's special chili, aside from these little firecrackers?"

Phil chuckled. "I start by browning some ground chicken in a bit of canola oil, then drain the fat off of it. I believe chili should take time to simmer, so I add it to a slow cooker with a couple tins of rinsed mixed beans, a drained can of sliced mushrooms, some chili-seasoned stewed tomatoes..."

As Phil continued to explain his recipe, he turned to face Maggie. At that moment, she leaned up, wrapped her arms around him, and kissed the writer full upon his lips. His eyes grew large in shock at the feel of her mouth upon his. Maggie broke away from the kiss, and apologized.

"I'm sorry," she said. "That was rather forward of me."

Phil inhaled deeply. "Yes, I'd say it was. Excuse me one moment, I have to powder my nose."

The writer walked out of the kitchen, and headed to the

bathroom. All my neighbor could think about was wondering if she had made a terrible mistake.

~ * * * ~

After washing his hands, Phil splashed some water upon his face. He was taken aback from what had happened. While he thought Maggie was a nice woman, for her to brazenly smooch him upon his lips was something he was not expecting.

"What the hell is going on with Maggie?" he asked himself.

A female voice answered him from behind the shower curtain. "Isn't it obvious, Phil?" it said. "She's got it bad for you."

The writer has a perplexed look on his face. He stared into the mirror, and didn't see anyone standing behind him. But, he heard the voice coming from beside him. He cautiously turned towards the shower, and pulled the curtain aside. Standing before him, in the stall, was the ghostly figure of Karen Prairie.

"Ugh," the specter bemoaned. "I've got to stop revealing myself in washrooms. They're the most uncomfortable places to be in."

"For yourself, or the person who is seeing you? Because right now, I'm about to drop one in my shorts."

"Please don't, Phil. I might be dead, but there's no need to be scared shitless of me."

The writer peered closer at my former fiancée. "Karen, is that you?"

Karen smirked. "Why, are there any other ghosts you see aside from me in Gary's shower? Could you be a dear, and help me out?"

Phil held the curtain open while Karen stepped out of the confined space. "I've heard about you appearing before Gary and Jessica in the past, but why are you doing so in front of me now?"

Kawartha Christmas Caper

"Because there is a wonderful woman in your kitchen right now who is completely enamored with you, and you're stuck in here wondering why in the world did she kiss you."

"Can you blame me, Karen? I thought Maggie was someone who is feeling vulnerable right now because her Christmas was stolen from her. I know she's looking for comfort, but I'm not sure if I'm the right guy to be providing that."

"Are you sure about that? Because she seems to think you fit the bill. Or, are you still hung up about the number Amy did on your head and heart last year?"

Phil was taken aback from the specter's bluntness. He knew from my reports she was the outspoken type, but this was the first time he had experienced it up close and personal. Now that he was able to see and hear her, he noticed my former fiancée was the type of woman who pulled no punches. She forced the writer to look within himself, and get in touch with his psyche.

"She hurt me bad, Karen. I know you and Gary loved each other."

"And, in somewhat morbid way, we still do."

"Nevertheless, Amy and I didn't share the same feelings and emotions the two of you do. Did I love Amy? Absolutely. But, when the person you love tells you right to your face those feelings aren't mutual? That's a dagger right through the heart."

"But, that was over a year ago. You've said yourself she has moved on. Isn't it time you did the same?"

Phil sighed. "I know I should. I'm not sure if I'm ready to, though."

A knock came upon the bathroom door. Maggie asked, "Phil, are you alright in there?"

"Just finishing up, Maggie," he replied.

Karen patted Phil's shoulder. "We'll talk later, but please, don't shut Maggie out entirely. She seems to have a good heart."

Phil nodded to the specter, and she vanished into thin air. The writer took a deep breath, opened the door, and saw my neighbor standing before him with a concerned look upon her face.

"Phil," Maggie started, "I want to apologize for being too forward. I shouldn't have kissed you so brazenly."

Phil was about to open his mouth when he heard Karen whisper in his ear, "Give her a chance."

The writer composed himself. "It's alright, Maggie," he said. "I'll admit I was taken aback by your forwardness, but it's something I'm not used to."

Maggie was still worried. "I hope you're willing to forgive me."

Phil smiled. "I know this is going to sound cliché, but 'it's not you, it's me.' Let's go into the living room, and I'll explain."

Maggie had a confused look on her face, but she followed the writer to the couch where they sat down. He spilled his story regarding not only Amy, but his believed true love from years before, Amber. A few tears were shed from Phil as he remembered how close he was to the Calgary lass. Maggie sat attentively as she heard Phil pour his heart and soul out.

Once he finished, he dried his eyes, and looked at my neighbor. "That's why I was shocked when you kissed me. I haven't felt that kind of love from a woman, save from a family member, for a long time."

"I'm sorry you haven't had much love in your life recently. No wonder you were uncomfortable by my attention."

"Don't get me wrong, Maggie. You appear to be a wonderful woman. But, I'm worried about your motives behind the interest."

44

Kawartha Christmas Caper

My neighbor grew alarmed. "Hold on, are you suggesting I'm 'not right in the head' because I'm developing an interest in you?"

"No, no," Phil clarified. "I'm only saying I'm concerned you might be feeling vulnerable right now after the robbery, and you're looking to me as a security blanket; someone who can make you feel safe during this time of despair."

Maggie rubbed her arm, and sighed. "I guess it could be thought of as such. I don't have much to be festive about right now. But, for some reason, in all of this craziness, I feel comfortable around you."

It was the writer's turn to be puzzled. "Okay, now I'm confused. You 'feel comfortable around' me?"

Maggie explained how she was an introvert; a person who tended to keep to herself, and didn't like socializing. She described how she would shy away from certain functions at the university. It was because of this type of personality, she admitted, she had remained single for many years. Yet, because of the calm energy Phil seemed to emit, her anxiety was not flaring up. That was why she decided to pursue the writer, in hopes the two of them were compatible.

Phil took Maggie's hand into his. "I don't know if things are going to work out between us; it's too early to tell," he said. "I'm the type of guy who tries not to rush into things because I've been hurt before. But, one thing I do know is I enjoy spending time with you, and if you're willing to be patient with me, I would like the chance to start a relationship."

My neighbor smiled. "I would like that," she replied.

The couple returned to the kitchen, and Phil resumed preparing his chili for the night's dinner. Maggie assisted when she could, but the writer did the majority of the work. Despite all of the chaos which had transpired a few days before, Maggie had begun to find her solace, and she found it in the form of my guest for the holidays. Phil's only concern was if Maggie would still be welcoming when she learned of his addiction.

CHAPTER 9

The entire drive back to my cottage from the O.P.P. detachment,
I was still fuming from Sgt. Betchel's decision to give us the rest
of the night off from the case. Jessica did her best to try to calm
me down, but she was fighting a losing battle. Fortunate for her,
a familiar ghostly voice of reason would add her two cents to the
situation.

"I'm going to take a stab in the dark here," Karen presumed,
"and, guess there was an edict Gary didn't care for?"

"Is there a time when he isn't pissed off because of one?" Jessica
posed.

"Not funny, gals," I responded.

"Look, Gary," my partner continued, "I'm not pleased with the
decision either. I'd love more than anything to raid Dryden's
residence right now, too. However, our hands are tied until the
morning when we can get the search warrant."

"I still think it's unfair we can't get one tonight, and conduct the
raid right away," I bemused.

"That's the problem with jurisdictions outside of major
metropolitan areas," Karen commented. "They go at a different
pace than the ones we're accustomed to."

"Be it as it may," I opined, "this still leaves the door open for
Dryden to unload some of his stash, if not skip town entirely. It's
a risk the Sargent is forcing us to take."

Jessica nodded. "I'll admit it is a gamble," she stated. "He's
forcing us to put some level of trust in a suspect, and we all
know someone with the rap sheet Dryden has can't be trusted."

"What kind of offenses are we dealing with here, aside from the
ones I already know about?" Karen quizzed.

"Take your pick," I answered. "Narcotic trafficking, weapon

possession; Dryden is a real work we're dealing with here."

"And yet," the specter observed, "you're planning on conducting a search of his property with the two Constables? Don't you think that's a large undertaking for such a small faction?"

"That was Sgt. Betchel's concern," Jessica noted. "He's worried we're biting off more than we can chew."

"As much as you two might not like to hear it," Karen commented, "I'm inclined to agree with him."

Jessica and I looked at each other, then gazed at the ghostly figure in my backseat through my rear-view mirror.

"Think about it, you two," the specter continued. "You're venturing into an area you're not familiar with, and with two officers who are a little green behind the ears. Plus, we all know Gary's history of finding his way into a hospital bed in some capacity. A rural property of undetermined acreage owned by a wing-nut with firearms in his possession? Sounds like more than a four-person job, if you ask me."

I sighed at the realization. We were about to embark on a huge undertaking, and we were planning on doing so on unfamiliar turf. Yes, I knew of some of the area via my treks to the cottage, but this was an area of Cottage Country I had not traveled to. Sgt. Betchel, as well as Constables Kassian and Jenner, had a better read on the territory, and both Jessica and I needed to put some trust in their judgment. It was something I was not proud of doing, having to resign some level of power and control, but the fact of the matter was, this was their jurisdiction, not ours. Jessica and I were merely assistants on the case, and it was the young Constables' collar.

Jessica broke the silence. "I guess you have a point there. We were used to doing things like we normally do in Toronto, and there is a different pace as to how things get done up here."

I agreed, "We do need to be mindful of our counterparts. They have more experience of the territory around here than we do;

the inner workings of getting warrants, and the ilk. All we can do is trust the Sargent's judgment, and hope to hell Dryden doesn't skip off with his loot."

"Just take it easy tonight, you two," Karen assured. "Rest up, and enjoy a hot meal back at the cottage."

"I'm not sure if Gary is up for cooking tonight after our roadblock with the Bewdley O.P.P.," my partner doubted.

"No worries," the specter commented. "Phil's taking care of it."

I turned the car sharply, and began to head towards Millbrook.

"Gary," Jessica exclaimed, "what the hell are you doing?"

"Trust me on this," I replied. "Given what I know of Phil's palate, if he's cooking dinner for us, we're going to need some pink bismuth."

~ * * * ~

After my detour to the drug store in Millbrook, Jessica and I pulled up to my cottage. Once exiting my vehicle, we were welcomed with the aroma of Phil's cooking.

"What is that smell?" Jessica quizzed.

"Let me see if I can detect it," I replied. I began to sniff the air. "Hmm, chicken, cumin, peppers... oh, no."

"What's wrong?"

"It's a good thing I made that trip; Phil's made his notorious chili."

We entered my abode, and were greeted by Benny, who was more than happy to see us. Phil came out from the kitchen to welcome us. "Hey, guys," he said. "I hope you didn't mind, but I figured you had a busy day working the beat, so I went ahead and began to prepare dinner for us."

"We smelt it when we got out of the car," Jessica commented.

"I hope you didn't make it too spicy this time," I worried.

"Now, Gary," Phil noted, "you know I like my chili on the bold side."

"Phil," I countered, "your chili is more than bold. The last time I tried it, the paint was coming off my bathroom in strips."

The writer laughed. "Don't worry, I decided to tame it down a tad this time. I got the hint after Maggie scorched her gullet on one of the Bird's Eye Chilies I normally put in it, so I decided to forgo them this time around."

Jessica raised her eyebrow. "Oh ho, so the two of you have been spending some time together?" she queried.

"We have," Phil confirmed. "I gave her an early Christmas gift, and in return, she took me into Peterborough to get the stuff for dinner tonight."

"Phil," I warned. "You didn't take advantage of my neighbor during this trying time for her, did you?"

The writer was taken aback by my questioning. "What? No!" he defended. "I only gave her a digital music file for her computer. Get your mind out of the gutter. Sheesh!" The oven timer went off. "Now, if you'll excuse me, I have to fetch the garlic bread before it burns." Phil walked off towards the kitchen.

Jessica giggled. "Guess he told you," she admonished.

"Okay," I reasoned, "so, I wasn't correct on that one."

I could hear Karen quip from the corner of the living room. "Wouldn't be the first time you were wrong."

~ * * * ~

Kawartha Christmas Caper

Jessica and I took our seats at my kitchen table, and Phil brought over a bowl of his chili for the three of us. Accompanying the meal was a basket of sliced garlic bread, which he placed in the center of the table. As we ate, we filled our friend in on how our day had gone with the crew at the Bewdley O.P.P. detachment. Like my partner and I were originally, Phil was dismayed over the news we had to wait until tomorrow for us to continue forth with the investigation.

"You mean to tell me even after you got a positive I.D. from the security footage, you have to wait until tomorrow to get a warrant?" he posed. "That doesn't make any sense."

"That's what we thought, too," I mentioned. "But, unlike in Toronto, they aren't as easily obtained around here."

Jessica agreed. "It is a setback," she added. "But, we have to play by the rules around here. We're not proud of having to do so, but such as the case."

"Hopefully," Phil mused, "things will run smoothly tomorrow, and you'll be able to conduct that search."

"We hope so, as well," I noted. "We're only concerned about a possible altercation between ourselves and the suspect. This guy's got a serious rap sheet attached to him."

"That's always a chance an officer takes in such scenarios," the writer observed.

Out of the corner of my eye, I saw Karen make her way over to the pot where the remainder of Phil's chili was sitting on the stove. She grabbed a spoon, and took a taste. "Mm," she commented. "Even without those chili peppers, it still packs quite a kick, but with a touch of sweet to it."

Phil responded, "That's the secret ingredient: strong-brewed Southwestern chai tea."

Jessica and I looked at each other, stunned. Did we just hear what we thought we heard?

51

"Um, Phil," Jessica asked. "Were you just talking to Karen?"

The writer nodded. "I was," he answered.

"Okay," I interjected, "I know you knew she existed, but when the hell did she reveal herself to you?"

Phil finished a bite of garlic loaf. "This afternoon," he replied. "She gave me some advice regarding Maggie."

"It's true," the specter confirmed. "I did. The woman was smitten with Phil, but he was feeling gun-shy after the whole mess with Amy, so I told him to give her a chance, and the rest was history."

Jessica probed, "Please tell me you didn't introduce yourself to Phil the same way you introduced yourself to me."

Karen stated, "All I will say is the Ladies' Washroom at the Division is a lot more spacious than the bathroom here at the cottage."

The four of us laughed at the revelation, and Phil told Jessica and me about the circumstances leading up to Karen's appearance before the writer.

"Hold on," Jessica interrupted. "Maggie kissed you?"

"Yep," Phil confirmed. "After she nearly burned her mouth off eating one of the Bird's Eye chili peppers I had originally gotten for dinner tonight."

"I guess that was quite a hot kiss in more ways than one," I mused.

"Seriously, Gary?" the specter admonished.

"Not cool, dude," the writer added. "The main thing is her taste buds weren't scorched too badly due to the pepper's spiciness. But despite that, Maggie and I had a nice chat about my past, and we're both on the same page now."

"So," Jessica inquired, "does this mean Phil has found a new woman in his life?"

The three of us looked at the writer, but he decided to keep his cards close to his chest. "I appreciate the interest," Phil answered. "But, a true gentleman doesn't kiss and tell."

No one said a word, but the look on Karen's face confirmed my partner's suspicion.

CHAPTER 10

My alarm sounded off at eight o'clock the next morning. I was reluctant to roll out of bed, but a lick of my face from Benny forced me to get up. I was about to head into the bathroom to shave and shower, only to find it occupied. A look towards Phil's room found his door was still closed, and he was snoring away. That meant Jessica was awake, and getting ready. I made my way to the kitchen to feed my husky his morning kibble, and put a pot of coffee on. Just as I was about to fetch the tin of coffee from the cupboard, my partner emerged from her hiding place dressed in a red turtleneck sweater, and black pants. She made a motion to kiss my cheek, and I attempted to beg off.

"Please," I requested, "not until I've had my morning coffee."

"You're not much of a morning person, are you?" Jessica countered.

"At least I'm up at this hour; unlike our house guest, who is still asleep."

"Give him a break, Gary. He's enjoying his vacation; something we're supposed to be doing, too."

"I know, I know. I'm to blame for that. 'Me, and my volunteering our services for this case.' I only hope we can find something at Dryden's place today, so we can nail him on a few charges."

"You and me, both. Dryden is a scourge on what is supposed to be a happy time for many. I would do anything to throw him behind bars."

As the coffee began to brew, I heard some rustling from the back bedroom. A few moments later, Phil began to trudge himself out to the kitchen. He was dressed in a gray hooded sweatshirt, and blue jeans.

"Oh, my God," Jessica jovially exclaimed, "he's alive!"

"Very funny, Detective Amerson," he scowled, taking a seat at the kitchen table. "I was having a rather odd dream before the aroma of brewed coffee roused me awake."

I grabbed three mugs from my cupboard. "Care to share, buddy?" I asked.

Phil recounted, "I can't remember the entire dream, but what I do recall involved me in a Santa suit."

"Really," I posed. "You don't suppose it was something regarding to a volunteer position you might have during the holidays in the future?"

The writer accepted a hot mug of Joe. "Who knows? The thing is I don't think I could ever see myself in such a role."

"How do you figure?" Jessica queried. "You seem like a jolly guy for the most part."

"Thanks for the compliment," Phil replied. "But, the truth of the matter is while I don't mind most kids, those who scream, yell, and carry on are the ones who grate on my nerves."

Jessica laughed. "I think that's the case with most adults," she commented.

"Be it as it may," the writer stated, "it seemed a little out of place for me to dream that." He turned to me. "What's your take on it, Gary?"

"I'm not willing to deduce anything about that," I said. "Knowing my current state, I'd probably infer it would tie into your budding relationship with Maggie, and I would get smacked upside the back of my head by either of the gals."

"Speaking of gals," Phil quizzed. "I'm surprised Karen hasn't offered her two cents on the situation."

"She doesn't show up all the time, Phil," Jessica explained. "She'll probably chime in when we're at the Detachment."

I reached up into the cupboard again for a bag of Quick Oats. "I'm going to make some oatmeal for breakfast," I announced. "Do either of you two want some?"

"I know I do," Phil replied. "I can't go the morning on coffee alone."

"If we're going to be searching Dryden's property," Jessica added, "I better have some, too."

I prepared the rest of the meal for the three of us, adding some brown sugar and cinnamon to the simmering pot. The meal was a good warm-up for a cold December morning, and helped provided the fuel Jessica and I needed for our day ahead. Phil cleaned up after breakfast, and told us he would hold down the fort while we were out on the beat. However, knowing the record Dryden had, we weren't sure if we would make it back in one piece.

~ * * * ~

Jessica and I arrived at the Detachment at quarter after ten in the morning, and we made a beeline straight for Sgt. Betchel's office. He was not pleased with our slight tardiness.

"Detectives," he greeted. "So glad you could join us this morning."

"Our apologies, Sargent," Jessica replied. "It's more difficult to get up some mornings than others."

"I take responsibility for that," I added. "We have a guest staying at my cottage for Christmas."

"Be it as it may," Sgt. Betchel stated, "I've been waiting for your arrival to brief you on the Dryden case."

"So, what are the latest developments?" I inquired.

The Sargent informed us he was successful in obtaining a search warrant for the Dryden property. However, much to his chagrin, he was unable to round up additional officers to accompany Jessica, me, and Constables Jenner and Kassian. Sgt. Betchel was hoping for a larger operation to storm the estate, in the event there would be a possible showdown between our forces and Dryden. But, despite his concerns, Jessica and I assured the Sargent we would do our best to obtain as much evidence as possible to further build our case against Dryden without incident. Yet, we could tell our temporary superior was not convinced. After we left the Sargent's office, a familiar voice chimed in with her two cents on the situation.

"I know you two don't like to hear it," Karen said, "I'm inclined to agree with Sgt. Betchel."

"You don't think the four of us could handle this operation?" I quizzed.

"I think you guys are perfectly capable of doing so," the specter clarified. "My concern is if Dryden shows up on the scene."

"I'll admit I'm worried about it, too," Jessica commented. "But, that's the risk Gary and I are willing to take."

Karen was unconvinced. "Okay," she warned. "But remember, there are two other officers working on this case. You're going to have to sell them on the decision it'll only be you four going up there. Don't forget, they were hesitant about such a small operation."

"We're aware of that," I replied. "It's going to be a tough pitch, but if we have any chance of recovering some of the stolen merchandise, we need to get up there ASAP."

We made our way over to the two Constables' desks, and informed them about what Sgt. Betchel had told us. Like Karen feared, they were not too pleased with the lack of backup on the operation. However, Jessica and I did our best to sell them on the fact it would be a huge boon to their young careers if we could nail Dryden on his laundry list of charges. Both Jenner and Kassian were still unsure about our operative, but time was ticking away, and we needed to act quickly. Any further delays, and the chance to raid the property undetected would be lost. Just like Constables Jenner and Kassian, I was hoping not to come face-to-face with Dryden, at least not at the current juncture. However, I was prepared to take that gamble, hence why I advised the two Constables to strap on some Kevlar, just to be on the safe side. But, sometimes my best intentions are not always met with favorable results.

~ * * * ~

The cloud cover was beginning to break apart, allowing the sun to shine down on the shores of Rice Lake. Phil was walking along the side road leading to my cottage with Benny for a daily constitutional. The winter nip in the air was the type of weather my husky enjoyed, but my writer friend was bundled up in a green winter jacket, accompanied with a blue scarf, black gloves, and a red knit hat. While he agreed to give Benny his necessary exercise, Phil cursed the fact he had to do so in such frigid conditions. It was by sheer fortune, Phil and Benny would soon find a companion who joined them on this morning.

"Phil," a familiar voice called out. "Wait up!"

The writer paused with my husky, and turned towards the direction of said voice. He found Maggie speed-walking up the road being led by Biscuit. The Pomeranian was clad in a red and white doggie coat, and little red booties on her paws. Maggie was donned in a black winter coat with the hood pulled up. A blue winter hat was poking out from underneath the faux fur trim of the hood. Covering my neighbor's hands was a pair of those red mittens a popular department store chain sold to raise funds for Canadian Olympic athletes. A smile emerged upon Phil's face when he recognized his companion.

"I'm surprised you're out and about at this time of day," she commented. "I would've thought you'd be stuck indoors, doing some writing."

"I needed a bit of a break from my Netbook," Phil explained. "Plus, I agreed to keep an eye on Benny when Gary is working on the case.

"Any news on how the investigation is coming along?"

As they resumed their walk, Phil filled Maggie in on the developments, so far. He mentioned we were looking at investigating the estate of our suspect sometime today. A look of concern crept upon Maggie's face.

"I hope there's not an incident over there," she worried.

"I don't know if there will be, or not," the writer commented. "Gary's not necessarily the safest detective around, but I'm keeping my fingers crossed he and Jessica will come back tonight unscathed."

"He does have a knack for ending up in hospital, on occasion," Maggie mused. "But, with Jessica alongside him on the investigation, he might be able to avoid a holiday stint in the ICU."

"We can only hope," Phil replied. "But, like I always say, 'There are many guarantees in life. But, life, in itself, is never a guarantee.'"

My neighbor was impressed. "That's quite a profound philosophy. Did someone famous say that?"

The writer chuckled, "I don't think so. It's something I came up with myself; a mantra I developed as I've gone through different experiences through the years."

"I'm guessing those 'experiences' are relationship-related, based on what you've told me about Amber and Amy."

Phil nodded. "And, in other relationships I've been in. I've been jerked around by ex-girlfriends in my younger years."

"I know how you feel. I've had my heart broken a few times, myself. Some men can be such pricks."

"No argument from me there. There are some good guys out

there, but based on the stereotypes I've heard, they're few and far between."

Maggie began to smile. "Oh, I don't know. I seem to think there is a certain good guy not far from me right now."

Phil chuckled. "Well, I'm not sure about that. I mean, everyone has their flaws. But, I'm flattered you think I'm one of them."

Phil and Maggie looked at each other, as the sun shone down upon them. The writer pulled back the hood to my neighbor's coat, and drew his hand to her cheek; lightly caressing her skin with his gloved hand. Maggie carefully stood up on the toes of her boots, and wrapped her arms around Phil for support. He helped my neighbor by embracing her for additional stability. Soon, the new couple pressed their lips against one another for a kiss which warmed them both on the chilly day. Benny looked on, and barked his approval of the budding duo. Phil and Maggie broke away from their kiss, and laughed at my dog's reaction.

"I guess Benny approves of our new relationship," she noted.

"It does appear that way," Phil said aloud. But, in the back of his mind, he offered his appreciation to Karen for opening his mind to what was standing in front of him.

CHAPTER 11

Jessica and I, along with Constables Jenner and Kassian, made our way from the Detachment to a quaint side road which meandered along the shores of the Pigeon River. We inched down the road, as not to raise suspicion of Dryden should he be on the premises. We were fortunate enough where he was not at home when we pulled up to the residence. I was amazed at the appearance of the dwelling. Its outer walls were constructed in a cordwood-style; however, unlike most houses built in this style, there were corners to the structure. Therefore, the cordwood was cross hatched to maintain the integrity of the structure.

The Constables, my partner, and I got out of our vehicles, and decided to investigate the premises. Jenner and Kassian went inside Dryden's home, while Detective Amerson and I went to check out the detached garage towards the rear of the property; all the while we kept in constant radio contact with one another. Jessica and I cautiously proceeded to the structure which looked like a small arched enclosure. We checked the garage to see if there was an entrance other than the main door, but were unable to locate one. The main door was closed and padlocked.

"Any luck, Celdom?" Kassian queried.

"It appears the garage is secured," I informed. "What about you guys?"

"If we didn't know the rap sheet on Dryden already, I'd say he's a gun collector. There are a couple rifles crossed over his fireplace."

"Stay safe, Constable. We don't know if or when he's going to show up."

"Roger that. Any idea about how to get past your barrier?"

I cocked my revolver. "I think I have a solution." I shot a couple bullets into the padlock in a bid to blow it open. My volley turned out to be successful, as the restraint broke in two. I warned my partner, "Careful, Amerson. We don't know if this structure is booby-trapped."

Jessica nodded, and stood flush against the side wall to the structure. I rolled up the door, and revealed a huge stash of merchandise being stowed away. "Jackpot," I announced.

"What's going on, Celdom?" Kassian asked. "We heard a shot from outside."

"We found a nice cache of stolen wares in here," I responded. "I think we have enough evidence here to make some of these charges stick."

"Let me get some photos of this, Celdom," Jessica requested, as she pulled out her smartphone. "We'll need some proof, in the event Dryden decides to unload any of this before we arrest him."

"Good idea, Amerson. I'll keep an eye and ear out in case Dryden shows up."

Jessica started snapping away while I stood guard by the opened garage door. I maintained radio contact with Kassian and Jenner as they continued to investigate inside the house. Ten minutes later, I heard a vehicle headed down the side road. In a bid not to rouse suspicion, I stepped inside the garage, and pulled the door down behind me.

Jessica complained about the lack of natural light. "What the hell, Celdom?" she argued.

"I think we have a visitor," I answered before radioing my compatriots. "Celdom to Kassian, be on guard. We might have a buzzard coming home to roost."

"Shit, Dryden's coming?" he replied. "We've got to take cover right away."

"Might be an idea. Amerson and I are tucked away in the garage, but wanted to give you and Jenner the heads up."

Kawartha Christmas Caper

"Much appreciated, Detective."

I attempted to see if there was some sort of viewing medium where I could observe the front of the property from inside the garage. I was fortunate enough to notice a peephole to the left of the closed door. I peered through, and noticed a maroon-colored pickup truck pull into the driveway. A burly white male in his 30's climbed out of the driver's side. A tuft of red hair protruded from underneath the back of his black knit hat, and he sported a profound beard of the same color. The man was clad in a hunter's jacket, and dark blue jeans. A pair of beige construction boots adorned his feet. It was my first glimpse of Warren Dryden in the flesh, and by the look on his face, he was not pleased with our presence.

"Who the hell is on my property?" Dryden bellowed. "If it's any cops, you better start praying for mercy!" He noticed the broken lock on the ground in front of the garage. "Son of a bitch," he muttered before storming back to his truck.

"What's going on?" Jessica whispered.

"Dryden's heading back to his vehicle," I replied. "My guess it's to get a weapon of some sort. He knows someone's broken into the garage."

"Great, and we're holed up in here? You better draw your gun; otherwise, we're sitting ducks."

"I'm on it." I pulled my .22 from its holster, and stood guard. Dryden returned from the back of his truck, but he was not empty handed. He cocked a semi-automatic, and made his way towards the garage.

"Amerson, get down!" I commanded.

Jessica and I ducked for cover, as Dryden tugged on the garage door. However, he heard a noise coming from inside his house. My partner and I looked at each other, and we remembered: Jenner and Kassian.

"Constables, on guard" I ordered. "Dryden's heading your way, and he's packing."

No sooner than I uttered those words, Dryden opened fire on his home; shooting out the windows to the dwelling.

"Celdom," Jessica begged, "we've got to go after him."

"He's got a semi-automatic," I informed. "We need to do so carefully, or we'll be Swiss cheese."

"If we don't hurry, Jenner and Kassian will be just that."

I nodded, and made my way to the garage door. I opened the door, and surveyed the area. Dryden had already made his way inside the house, so we had to move quickly. With our guns drawn we attempted to scurry towards the dwelling; however, Dryden spotted us, and began to open fire in our direction. Jessica and I dove behind a stack of logs earmarked for firewood before returning fire. We exchanged volleys of bullets before Dryden ran out of ammo. The suspect dashed out of the house, and made a beeline for his pickup. I continued firing rounds in his direction, but he was able to get away.

Jessica had made her way into the domicile, and evaluated the scene. Shards of glass littered the carpet in front of the windows, and bullet holes could be seen in the walls and furniture. I joined my partner inside a few moments later, and exhaled.

"I'm going to gather he escaped," Jessica presumed.

"For a big guy," I commented, "he sure can motor."

"Were you able to get the plate to his truck?"

"Kind of hard to do that when you're firing a few rounds, but yeah, I got it down." I looked around the living room. "This sure looks like a disaster area."

Jessica looked into one of the back rooms, and shook her head. "Actually, it's a crime scene."

I came to investigate with her, and saw what we feared the most: the bullet-ridden corpses of Constables Jenner and Kassian. My partner and I stood there, and bowed our heads for our former comrades. The silence was broken by a familiar ghostly voice.

"Well," Karen remarked, "Sgt. Betchel is going to be pissed."

It turned out to be the biggest understatement of the entire week.

CHAPTER 12

A few hours later, after giving our reports to the Special Investigations Unit, Jessica and I found ourselves back in Sgt. Betchel's office, getting dressed down by our temporary superior.

"I knew this was a bad idea to send you four up there," he bemoaned.

"With all due respect, Sargent," I offered. "It was because you couldn't find the additional manpower to back us up on this assignment."

"Oh, shut up, Celdom," he spat. "It was your suggestion in the first place to raid his property when you knew full well what we were dealing with. I should never have let you talk me into it."

"If I may, Sargent," Jessica interrupted. "Detective Celdom and I knew we had to act quickly, or Dryden would have unloaded the merchandise we found on his property."

"Ah yes, the evidence," Sgt. Betchel continued. "The wares which have since been seized by the S.I.U. An investigation I wanted to keep within our jurisdiction, but now I have the higher-ups crawling all over our Region, and two dead cops. I dread having to tell their families their husbands and sons won't be home for Christmas because they're being buried."

"We both take full responsibility for what happened," I replied.

"And, so you two should," he fumed. "This is why big city policing should stay out of my area; people get killed."

"In all fairness, Sargent," Jessica opined. "Dryden's criminal record is forcing big city policing to encroach on the area. Drug trafficking, robberies, and now a double homicide? All of these are things we encounter on a daily basis in Toronto. Warren Dryden brought these problems into your jurisdiction, and we're doing our best to nip it in the bud before it becomes more widespread."

Sgt. Betchel leaned back in his chair, and absorbed what my partner had said. It was true, Peterborough County was a peaceful region nestled within Ontario's Eastern Cottage Country. However, with its close proximity to the Greater Toronto Region, certain aspects of the metropolis were creeping into the area. Warren Dryden was a prime example of the dark side of the coin. Jessica and I didn't want to be involved with any of this originally, but when Dryden made his presence known to us via Maggie, we knew we had to get involved; although, it was more from Phil's urging to do so. Now, Dryden had blue blood on his hands, and it made us more vigilant to get him behind bars.

"Do you two think you'll still be able to bring Dryden in?" the Sargent posed.

"Keep us on this case, and I know we will," my partner replied.

"Are you positive about that?" Sgt. Betchel quizzed.

"Sir," Jessica answered, "I bet my career on it."

I didn't say a word, but the expression on my face told a different story. Before I could dispute the promise, our temporary superior took Jessica's word.

"Alright, Amerson," Sgt. Betchel stated. "You're on. You and Celdom can continue on the case, but if you fail to get Dryden behind bars, I will do my damnedest to make sure you both lose your shields."

I attempted to argue my hesitance, but the Sargent wasn't going to have any of it. He ushered us out of his office, and told us to get back to work on the case. Jessica and I walked back to the desks of our fallen comrades, and she could tell I was not pleased with Sgt. Betchel's edict. It was something picked up by a familiar visitor, as well.

"That was a pretty ballsy proclamation you made there," Karen stated.

"Someone had to make it," Jessica reasoned. "I'm not happy with the fact Jenner and Kassian are dead."

"Neither was the Sargent," I added. "You saw how he tore a strip off of both of us. Lieutenant Davis was never that hard on you. Me, yes, but we all know my track record; it'd be natural for my career to be on the line. But, you have a long one ahead of you, Amerson. I don't want those bad traits of mine to rub off on you."

"I know you don't, Celdom," Jessica noted. "But, we have two dead officers as a result of our investigation. It's natural for both of us to receive flack because of what happened, but you can't tell me you don't want to nail Dryden, too."

"Believe me," I retorted, "I want this prick doing time in Millhaven as much as you do. However, we both know what Dryden is capable of. Are you sure you're willing to risk your career -- if not your life -- to try to bring him in?"

Jessica answered, "We can't have Dryden still roaming the countryside, robbing homes and businesses, and plugging anyone who gets in his way. He's ruined Christmas for a lot of families already. We need to stop him before he tarnishes the holidays for many more."

"Jessica," Karen interrupted, "I know your heart is in the right place, as I know Gary's is, too. But, you both have to remember this is one violent criminal you're dealing with. He's already gunned down two of your brethren, and there's no telling how many more he has killed, or will kill in the near future. Hell, what's not to say if it wasn't for Jenner and Kassian making all that commotion in his house it'd be you two in the morgue?"

"She does have a point," I agreed. "We were lucky to make it out of that garage unscathed. What's not to say we'll be as fortunate the next time we cross paths with him? Especially, when we know what sort of firepower he has access to."

My partner nodded. While Jenner and Kassian were not as fortunate, Jessica and I avoided the barrage of fire from a semi-automatic; a weapon not easily obtained in this neck of the woods. We figured Dryden had some ties to the gang culture in Toronto in order to get his hands on such weaponry, but we wanted to make sure. I decided to place a call to the Guns & Gangs Department back in Toronto to see if there were any connections between our suspect and the hoodlums back home. It was a conversation which triggered a reaction on both ends of the line.

~ * * * ~

Maggie was puttering around her kitchen; attempting to fix lunch for herself and her guest who was over at my cottage, settling Benny down after their walk from earlier in the day. A few minutes later, there was a knock upon Maggie's door, and Biscuit started yipping loudly. Maggie came to answer it, and a smile emerged upon her face when she recognized her visitor.

"Well, hello, Phil," she greeted.

"Afternoon, Maggie," the writer answered. The couple embraced, and kissed each other once again. "Mm, looks like someone missed me."

"Of course, I did. Is that so wrong?"

"Not really, but considering we last saw each other about an hour ago, one might think we're akin to two kids experiencing their first love."

"I repeat, is that so wrong?"

Phil laughed. "I don't think so, as long as we're both love each other, or at the very least, in serious 'like' with one another."

"Well, that is something I'm definitely experiencing."

The writer gave a confused look. "Definitely 'love', or definitely 'like'?"

Maggie smacked Phil, playfully. "Will you stop that? You know

I'm crazy about you."

"As am I, you. Just wanted to make sure after the whole Amy fiasco a couple years back."

"I understand that, but I want to assure you I will never toy with your heart like she did. I know you've had a rough go when it comes to prior relationships, but unless you intentionally hurt me, I am here to stay."

Phil wrapped his arms around Maggie. "I have no intentions to do that. I'll admit I'm not perfect; I have my flaws, but I will never consciously hurt you."

My neighbor smiled. "I appreciate that."

Maggie led the writer to the dining table where their lunch was already set up. The meal consisted of bowls of beef and vegetable soup with a thick broth, accompanied with sandwiches comprised chiefly of deli-sliced turkey breast and Provolone cheese for the filling. Phil complimented his host for the meal, but before the couple began eating, Maggie passed her guest an envelope.

The writer was perplexed. "What's this?" he inquired.

"It's a little something to say Merry Christmas," Maggie explained. "Also, since you gifted me the Peter Grossman Christmas song, I thought it was fair to give you something in return."

"Well, thank you kindly, then." Phil began to open the envelope.

"You're welcome. I hope you enjoy it."

Phil removed a greeting card from the envelope, and read the front of it. He smiled in appreciation for the gesture, which pleased his host. However, Phil's expression changed when he opened the card, and noticed what was inside: a gift pack of scratch-off lottery tickets.

70

"Oh, dear," he replied.

"What's wrong, Phil?" Maggie worried. "Don't you like it?"

"I appreciate the gesture, but unfortunately, I can't accept the gift."

"Why not?"

Phil took a deep breath. "Remember when I said earlier about not being perfect? This is one of the things I was referencing."

"What are you saying? Is someone in your family a problem gambler?"

Phil nodded. "There is, me."

Maggie's heart sank a little. "I'm sorry, I didn't know. How long has it been going on?"

Phil began to explain his battles with his addiction. He detailed how he started at a young age, but it exploded when he made his first trip to a slots-at-racetrack facility in Rexdale in 2000. He admitted he had been seeking counseling for his illness for the past two years. Phil also mentioned the time he was picked up for being thrown out of an off-track horse betting facility, but was let off with a warning after a stern lecture by Jessica and myself.

Maggie listened attentively, but began to doubt the prospect of a relationship with the writer. Here, she thought Phil was the perfect man for her; someone whom she felt comfortable with. However, the admission of having an addictive personality was a huge strike against him. Yes, he was someone seeking guidance in arresting his illness, but she worried how he might behave in the event of a relapse. How much out of control would he get if he were to slip? There was a bevy of questions she had for Phil; however, she was afraid he would grow upset with her barrage of queries.

Phil picked up on Maggie's concern, and invited her to ask as many questions as she desired. He answered each one of them honestly, and even confessed to not knowing all of the answers, yet was quick to reiterate he was willing to continue to work on his recovery. Phil stated the road to recovery had not been easy since he had been going through it alone, save for those who have attended group therapy sessions with him.

"However," he finished, "I hope to have some additional support along the way."

Maggie hesitated. "I don't know, Phil. I have quite a few trust issues from my past, and I'm afraid of what might happen if we were to proceed with our relationship, and you ended up going back to gambling."

Phil sighed. "I honestly don't know what would happen if I were to slip. Even if it was something as little as a $1 scratch ticket, that's still considered as such, and I would have to re-declare my start date of recovery. I just know I cannot gamble for anything. That's why I avoid a certain coffee shop every February and March."

"Hold on, are you telling me that contest where they have winning prize messages underneath the rim of the coffee cup is considered gambling?"

"If it leads to compulsive behavior, like buying more hot beverages from the chain than you normally would, then yes."

Maggie shook her head. "I never realized how much gambling is subconsciously ingrained in our culture."

"Believe me, as someone who has suffered from this for over 30 years, it can be quite scary. That's why I have to decline the gift pack."

"I understand, and I appreciate you telling me about this. You're not mad at me about this?"

Phil shook his head. "Nope, are you?"

Maggie exhaled. "Well, I'll admit I still have my concerns, but as long as you're still willing to continue therapy, and stay clean, then I can manage."

"Thanks for the understanding and support, Maggie. Now, let's get back to eating our lunch before our soup gets any colder. I don't think this is the type which is meant for Gazpacho."

Maggie laughed. "I don't think so either. Bon appetit."

The couple resumed dining, and would exchange loving glances with each other with the occasional bite. Phil felt relieved for admitting one of his biggest flaws to Maggie, and while she still was apprehensive, being able to discuss it with her enabled a better understanding of one another. Others might have seen it as a death knell for any budding relationship, but with the love and understanding Phil and Maggie shared, it was the beginning of the next chapter of their lives together.

CHAPTER 13

After my call with the Guns & Gangs Department in Toronto
both Jessica and I decided to pay Sgt. Betchel another visit.
Considering how we were both chewed out earlier, we dreaded
seeing him again in a short span of time. I knocked on his door
with caution.

"Come in," he invited.

My partner and I entered his office. "My apologies for the
intrusion, Sargent," I announced. "But, we just received some
information on the Dryden case."

"I hope this is better than the earlier developments at his estate."

"That depends on how you look at it."

I repeated what I had learned during my phone call to Guns &
Gangs Department. Dryden had ties to one of the most notorious
gangs in all of Toronto, the Malvern Crew. For years they had
been engaged in a turf war in Scarborough with their rivals, the
Galloway Boys. The two gangs had been involved in a bitter
shootout during a block party at a housing complex east of where
Phil lived 17 months prior, where 2 people were killed, and 22
others wounded. Sgt. Betchel rubbed his eyes and sighed. What
he feared had transpired in his jurisdiction, big city crime had
infiltrated the Kawarthas Region.

"So, where do we go from here?" he queried.

"The Guns & Gangs Department has been notified of the
murders of Constables Jenner and Kassian at the hands of
Dryden," Jessica reported. "They offer their sympathies."

"That offers little comfort, Amerson," the Sargent replied.

Jessica continued, "That being said, they will be working on their
end to assist us further in the investigation."

I could tell by the pained expression on Sgt. Betchel's face he was not impressed with further involvement by a big city police department. He was content with things being quiet and calm in his jurisdiction. Alas, that serenity had been shattered by the atrocities Dryden had committed. If we had any shot at getting the man who killed two of his officers, Sgt. Betchel would have to bite the bullet, and allow the Toronto P.D. more access to the investigation.

The Sargent sighed, "Well, I guess if this is the only way we can get Dryden behind bars, it has to be done. Just remember, this investigation is still in your hands. If you two fail to bring him in, I'll make damn sure you both lose your shields."

I nodded. "Yes, sir. You've made that perfectly clear from your reprimand earlier."

"Just wanted to make sure you haven't forgotten my warning, Celdom," he cautioned. "Now, back to work with you both."

"Thank you, Sargent," Jessica replied. My partner and I left the Sargent's office, and made our way back to our desks where Karen was awaiting us.

"He's still not impressed with the increased involvement of the big city police, huh?" the specter quizzed.

"Not really," Jessica commented. "And, he's even more steamed now there will be more of us getting into the investigation."

"It's a necessary evil," Karen mused. "But, the more officers on the case, the better the chance of nabbing Dryden."

"True enough," I observed. "But, by the same token, I can see where the Sargent is coming from."

Jessica blinked. "How do you figure?"

I explained, "Remember the adage, 'Too many cooks spoil the broth'? That's probably Sgt. Betchel's thinking. This is a pretty laid back jurisdiction, and Betchel is the same way in his duties. However, for a case of this magnitude, you need to pull out the big guns."

"Especially when there are two Constables dead at the hand of this psychopath," Karen added.

"Be it as it may," Jessica stated, "we have to think about where we should go from here. Dryden knows we're on his trail, so we have to presume he's going to try to unload some of that stolen merchandise we found in his garage."

"Jessica has a point," Karen agreed. "I don't know what the black market scene is out here, but you would think there would be some sort of exchange for goods Dryden could actually utilize."

"Like, drugs and firearms," I noted. "I'd like to punch into more resources here at the Detachment, but after what happened with Jenner and Kassian, I don't think Sgt. Betchel is willing to trust us with more of his men."

The three of us sat at my desk, attempting to wrack our brains for some semblance of an idea. However, sometimes such opportunities fall right into your lap.

~ * * * ~

Phil and Maggie walked down the road near her home with Benny and Biscuit leading the way. The writer dreaded having to venture out in the cold, but knew my husky needed his exercise, and figured it was best to do so before the sun went down for the day. However, he was appreciative of the human company he had for these recent constitutionals. Biscuit was thankful for the four-legged companionship, as well. The Pomeranian enjoyed having another canine to go out on her strolls with. The budding couple talked about various topics ranging from current events to their personal relationship histories. Phil learned Maggie had owned an array of small dogs in the past, but alas, due to old age, and other ailments, they had made their way across the so-called 'Rainbow Bridge'. Maggie spoke with emotion when she remembered her 'fur babies' of the past. The writer picked up on his companion's tone and facial expressions when discussing a particular breed.

"I'm guessing you would prefer to have another dog?" he observed. "One who could keep Biscuit company when you're at work?"

Maggie nodded. "I do. Don't get me wrong, I love Biscuit, but she's not someone who likes to cuddle with me in bed. I like being able to have a little critter to snuggle with me while I sleep."

Phil joked, "Well, that rules me out, then. I'm too big to nuzzle in your arms under the covers."

Maggie playfully smacked her companion's arm. "You know what I mean. But, that doesn't necessarily mean we couldn't snuggle one another sometime."

"In due time, Maggie. I don't want to make the same mistakes Gary has in the past when it's come to women."

My neighbor nodded. "Yes, I have noticed Jessica seems a little apprehensive when it comes to intimacy with him."

"I can't say I blame her, though. I mean, after Karen and Elaine, Jessica believes she will become another notch on Gary's bedpost if she does end up sleeping with him."

"But, Gary was engaged to Karen, so you really can't paint her with the same brush as Elaine."

"True enough, and Elaine was a real piece of work to begin with. She really did a number on Gary's head and heart. Thankfully, Jessica was there as his work colleague to help him through that trying time when Elaine was trying to woo Gary back."

Maggie blinked. "Jessica has been working with him for that long?"

"Apparently so. Gary said she was just starting out down at the Division when Elaine came to visit for the big annual Caribbean Festival with the guy she dumped Gary for."

My neighbor shook her head. "I can't believe she would do that; flaunting her new man in front of the old one."

Phil agreed. "And, doing it around the time of Gary's 50th, too. Elaine had no scruples whatsoever. Especially, when she showed her true colors by trying to win Gary back after Carlito was gunned down during the parade on the Saturday of the festival's final weekend. Fortunately, Gary came to his senses; thus, paving the way to the relationship he has now with Jessica."

"Just out of curiosity, you mentioned Amy was seeing someone new now. Do you think you'd fare any better if she trotted him out like a show pony in front of you, like Elaine tried to do with Carlito?"

Phil exhaled as he thought about the possibility. "That's hard to say. Amy screwed me over pretty bad. Honestly, I would like to think I could, but I wouldn't know for certain unless that were to happen. But, one thing is for certain, having a beautiful woman, like yourself, on my own arm would lessen the sting."

The couple leaned in for another kiss, but was broken up when Benny began tugging on his leash. Phil begged the husky, "Whoa, easy there, buddy." However, Benny took off like a shot, dragging Phil in tow. Maggie sighed, and ran after the two of them; attempting to catch up with Biscuit leading her. The two weren't looking for an afternoon jog, but Benny and Phil made sure they got some exercise, as well.

~ * * * ~

By the time Maggie and Biscuit had caught up with their walking companions, Maggie was short of breath. She would find Benny and Phil crouched down by a couple of snow-covered bushes, looking towards a cottage further down the road.

"Jeez, Phil," Maggie panted. "Give me a little more advance warning when you're going to take off like that."

The writer shushed his neighbor. "Don't blame me," he

whispered. "Benny must have sensed something, and took off for down here."

"I can see that, but why did he stop here?"

"That's what I'm trying to figure out."

Benny whined at Phil, and turned his head towards the cottage. The human couple focused their attention on the scene in front of them. Biscuit was becoming fidgety and was about to yip, but Maggie quickly covered her mouth. The last thing they needed was for the Pomeranian to blow their cover. Two men were seen getting out of a cube van, and were talking to one another. One man was stocky in build, the other was tall and lanky; both were dressed in black wool hats, and winter gear.

"So, what's the plan?" the tall individual asked.

"According to what Dryden said," the stocky man reported, "we're supposed to bring the van by his place at 9:30 tonight to load it up. He was insistent we bring his payment along with us."

"I'm surprised we were able to get this out of Toronto undetected. These are some serious firepower we've got in the back."

"Toronto P.D. aren't the smartest knives in the drawer. We've been running this shit for years, and they haven't caught up to us yet."

"Dumb-assed cops. They've put a few dents in our corps, but we're still going strong. Anyway, I'm going to grab a bite to eat, and rest up before we head over to Dryden's."

"Sounds like an idea, I'm famished."

The two goons headed into the cottage to further plot their evening ahead. Maggie and Phil emerged from their hiding places, and nodded to each other. They needed to get a hold of Jessica and myself to inform us of the latest developments. But first, they had to do it from safe harbor. Phil tugged on Benny's leash, and headed back to my place where the writer would place an important phone call.

CHAPTER 14

Jessica and I continued to sit at our desks, wracking our brains to attempt to figure out what Dryden's next move would be. I got up and made my way to the break room to fetch some coffee for my partner and me. When I arrived at the coffee machine, Karen was waiting for me to discuss the apparent stalemate we were in.

"This is a tough case to crack," the specter observed.

"You're telling me," I commented. "I suspect Dryden has decided to go into hiding after our exchange yesterday. The problem is we don't know where that might be. Common sense dictates he's going to unload his inventory of stolen merchandise, but we're at a dead end on that."

"Do you think he's had an opportunity to relocate his stash since the shootout?"

"That's hard to say. There was quite a bit in that garage. A moving truck, or van would be noticeable on that country road."

"Unless he did it under the cloak of darkness last night. That would make things less detectable."

"Possibly, but I don't think he could have organized such transport in a short time."

"Don't be too sure, Gary. Toronto's only a 90-minute drive away, and Dryden does have ties to the Malvern Crew. What's not to say he could have rallied his gang associates to orchestrate a quick exchange?"

I stood there, and thought about Karen's suggestion. While it did seem unlikely on a quick observation, it made logical sense. Dryden knew we were hot on his trail, and he would want to get rid of any evidence he had; in this case, the huge stash he had accumulated. But, who would he liquidate it to, and for what? Cash, drugs, or more firearms? There were so many options he could barter the goods for, all of them viable and could easily be obtained by the Malvern Crew. The only questions I still had

Douglas J. McLeod

were when and where such an exchange would take place.

I returned to my desk with the cups of Joe for Jessica and myself where I found my partner finishing up an important phone call.

"Who was that?" I queried.

"That was Phil," she informed. "He and Maggie stumbled upon a hot tip. Dryden's going to unload the stolen goods tonight at his place to a couple Malvern Crew members for firearms."

"I guess I better inform Sgt. Betchel about these latest developments. Amerson, get on the phone to the Guns and Gangs Unit back in Toronto, and see if they can send some backup for the exchange tonight. If we have a shot at nailing them, we need to jump on this as quickly as possible."

Jessica picked up the phone again. "I'm on it, Celdom."

I made a beeline to the Sargent's office to fill him in on our plan, hoping he would give us the proper support to do so.

~ * * * ~

"Are you sure about this tip, Celdom?" the Sargent asked.

"Yes, sir," I confirmed. "We have a couple of witnesses who stumbled upon a cottage by Rice Lake where a couple members of the Malvern Crew were discussing the exchange at Dryden's residence tonight."

Sgt. Betchel shook his head in disbelief. "That doesn't seem like a smart decision on his part."

"With all due respect, sir, the Malvern Crew are one of the most notorious gangs in Toronto. The notion Dryden is associated with him ought to be disturbing for all of us. What's more, the fact there would be firearms exchanged for his pilfered merchandise makes the situation more alarming for every resident and merchant in the Kawarthas."

82

"And, how do you suggest we approach the situation? The last time you went to Dryden's residence, two of my men were gunned down."

"Detective Amerson is on the phone to Toronto to organize some reinforcements for the operation tonight. We hope there will be enough officers on hand to prevent a repeat of the other day."

Jessica joined us a couple minutes later, and informed us of the developments.

"I just got off the phone with the Guns and Gangs Unit in Toronto," she announced. "They will be sending about 25 members of the Unit to try to nab Dryden and his associates tonight."

"Excellent, Amerson," the Sargent commended.

"Will there be any contribution of officers from here who will be joining in the operation?" Jessica queried.

"I don't know," Sgt. Betchel hesitated. "I'm a little anxious after the last time you two headed up there."

"That was because we didn't have the reinforcements as we do now," I mentioned. "If you recall, the last time we visited Dryden's residence, there were only four officers on hand. Tonight, we have the opportunity to have seven times those numbers. We could add more to those if we had other Constables joining us on the mission."

Sgt. Betchel thought about it for a moment. Both Jessica and I knew he was still holding us responsible for the deaths of Constables Jenner and Kassian, and we could see the reluctance in his face. However, on the flip side, we could tell he did not want this to be a Toronto-dominant operation. The Sargent wanted some O.P.P. Bewdley involvement, but wasn't sure if he could afford more dead officers under his command. Yet, if he were to offer some officers to the operation, there would be some additional protection for them with the increased police presence from the Toronto P.D. Guns and Gangs Unit.

The larger support net from the big city was appealing, but it still ate at Sgt. Betchel. He had made it clear in the past he was not pleased with others interfering with his jurisdiction. By Jessica and myself volunteering our services, we had gone against the Sargent's belief system. It ended up opening a huge can of worms in his opinion. Now, there was going to be a larger outside police presence in his backyard. He hated the notion, but in order to get Dryden behind bars, it was the only option he had left.

"Alright," he conceded. "I'll see if I can scratch up a few of my men to assist in the operation. But remember, Detectives, my earlier edict still stands: if any of them get killed, I'm going to do my damnedest to have your badges."

"We understand, sir," Jessica commented. "We might have let you down the other day, but now we have strength in numbers. We'll make sure your men will return back safe."

"You have our word, Sargent," I added.

We were dismissed from Sgt. Betchel's office, and we grabbed coats.

"A quick bite before we head up to Dryden's place?" I suggested.

"I'm for that," my partner nodded. "Hopefully, it won't end up being a last meal for us."

~ * * * ~

The only problem with being in the middle of nowhere is the fact getting out to eat requires a drive. Considering Bewdley is a small hamlet, the only options to go out to a restaurant are to either go to Millbrook, or the larger city in the area, Peterborough. Knowing we would be pressed for time, we opted to drive to the closer Millbrook in hopes to find something. Jessica and I were fortunate enough to find a quaint family restaurant there. The establishment was adorned with decorations to celebrate the festive season, and was busy with regular patrons. My partner and I were seated, and perused the menus. A few minutes later we were joined by Maggie and Phil which would have surprised me had Jessica not invited them before we left the Detachment.

"Hey, guys," Phil greeted. "Have you been waiting long?"

"We just sat down," I announced.

"Have you eaten here before, Maggie?" Jessica quizzed.

"Not really," my neighbor answered. "Whenever I've gone out to eat, it has usually been to some place in Peterborough with my co-workers. Otherwise, I order in, or throw something in the microwave."

I chuckled. "Well, if you get Phil to move in with you, he could help change that." I soon felt the pain of Phil kicking my shin from underneath the table.

"Easy there, Gary," the writer cautioned. "Maggie and I are just starting our relationship. There's no need to rush into anything, unlike others at this table have been apt to do."

Somehow, I could hear Karen snickering, and muttering, "Burn!"

"Besides," Phil continued, "my family have been trying to get me to move up here for years."

Maggie blinked. "You make it sound like that would be a bad thing."

"Don't get me wrong," the writer clarified. "The Kawarthas are a very nice and beautiful region, but it doesn't offer all of the things Toronto has in the terms of entertainment options."

Jessica agreed. "He does have a point. There are a few museums, theaters, and sports options where one could go in Toronto. For anything around here, one would have to trek to Peterborough to enjoy anything resembling those."

"But, I will give the region credit for one thing," Phil noted. "It is a wonderful place to get away from the craziness of the big city. The picturesque scenery has been a boon for my writing, as has the company this week."

The writer took Maggie's hand into his, and kissed the back of it. My neighbor smiled and blushed due to her beau's gallant action. The waitress came by to take our orders. Jessica and I settled for a couple club sandwiches, Maggie opted for a burger and fries, and Phil chose a hot beef sandwich. The four of us continued the casual chat until we were served our meals. Phil surveyed the restaurant to make sure the two individuals didn't stop in for dinner themselves. When he noticed the coast was clear, the writer nodded to me to open up the discussion about what he and Maggie stumbled upon earlier in the afternoon.

However, we decided to keep our cards close to our chest to make sure no one else overheard our conversation. This was akin to a massive sting, and the last thing we needed was the media to interfere with the planned bust. Instead, Maggie talked about a Christmas party for her University colleague's children early on Christmas Eve. It was an annual event her work threw, but was thrown into disarray with Dryden's antics. Jessica and I assured Maggie we would do our best not to have our suspect ruin the festivities by locking him away behind bars before then. My partner noticed my neighbor was trying to tell Phil something, but was not sure how to approach the subject.

"Is there something eating at you, Maggie?" Jessica quizzed.

Maggie nodded. "There is. Our normal Santa has been battling the flu for the past few days."

"It is a nasty strain going around this year," I commented.

"Anyway," my neighbor continued, "I was wondering if there was a certain someone who could fill in for him?"

I patted my stomach. "I would need to pad the suit a little."

"Sorry, Gary," Maggie corrected. "I was thinking of our other male companion for the role."

Phil nearly choked on his food. "Me?" he asked. "You want me to play Santa?"

"Why not?" Jessica countered. "You would be the perfect Saint Nick."

"I agree," I added. "This would be a wonderful opportunity for you."

"I don't know," the writer hesitated. "I'm not that good with little kids."

"Please, Phil?" Maggie begged. "I'm being saddled with playing Mrs. Claus for the party. If you would do this for me..." Then, Maggie whispered something in his ear.

Without any further delay, Phil grinned. "What time do you need me on Christmas Eve?"

CHAPTER 15

After we finished our dinner out, Maggie and Phil headed back to her place for the evening. Phil wished Jessica and me the best of luck in our operation later that night. I always found it odd for Phil to do so, considering his addiction; however, I knew he meant it as an expression, and hoped it wasn't a subtle trigger for himself somewhere down the line. My partner and I debated about what it was Maggie whispered in his ear which sold him on the Santa gig. Jessica speculated it to be a special gift Maggie would give the writer, but I attempted to discount it, citing Phil not to be type of person who would "give himself unto a woman" so easily. A familiar ghostly voice begged to differ.

"Trust me, Gary," Karen disputed. "The majority of men would leap at the opportunity should it be presented to them."

"And, as proof," Jessica added, "I present Exhibit 'A'." My partner gestured towards me.

I sighed. "You two are never going to let me live that down, are you?"

"Not in a million years, dear," the specter quipped.

"Regardless," I countered, "Maggie doesn't strike me as the type of person who would suggest that to Phil. She knows he's still smarting from the Amy situation. Why would she put that on the table now?"

"Isn't it obvious, Gary?" Jessica stated. "She doesn't know if Phil will be back up this way again. This is an attempt for her to stake her claim on him."

Karen agreed. "It's similar to you and Elaine."

I argued, "Okay, first of all, I saved Elaine's life before all of that shit happened in Barbados."

"He does have us there," the specter said to my partner.

"And, second," I continued, "It's a hell of a lot easier for Phil to see Maggie on a regular basis than it was for Elaine and me."

Jessica resigned, "Okay, so a 90-minute drive is easier than a 6-hour flight; I'll grant you that. But, in case you haven't noticed, Maggie is really into Phil."

"And, Phil likes Maggie," I disputed. "But, I don't think it's on the same level as she likes him."

Karen queried, "So, you're telling me Phil will chicken out at the last minute once they get back to her place after the party?"

"I don't know," I said. "I can't speak for him. But, I'm not going to press him on the matter. Phil and Maggie are their own couple, and if either of them want to volunteer that information, that's up to them. Otherwise, it's none of my business."

The ladies lowered their heads and conceded I was right for once. While Phil and Maggie were our friends, it was unprofessional of us to partake in gossip about them; especially after they had given us a hot tip regarding our case. I checked my watch, and suggested we head back to the Detachment to meet up with the Unit coming up from Toronto before heading to Dryden's place for the hopeful showdown and capture.

~ * * * ~

After meeting up with the Guns and Gangs Unit officers at the O.P.P. Detachment in Bewdley, we made our way to Dryden's home outside of Bailieboro. We had to be discreet in our stakeout positions, as it was a narrow side road along the shores of the Pigeon River. We were thankful Dryden's neighbors were gracious enough for us to set up camp on their property; otherwise, the operation would have been more difficult to execute. Jessica and I stood guard in our vehicle, observing Dryden's property through what little cover could be found at this time of year near the residence.

"Base Camp to Lone Wolf," my CB Radio crackled. "Are you guys in position, over?"

"Lone Wolf to Base Camp," I responded. "We're near the Hen House, keeping an eye on the festivities. It's quiet for now, but we'll let you know when something comes up, over."

"10-4."

Jessica looked on through a set of binoculars. "You sure this is going to work, Celdom?" she worried.

"It has to, Amerson," I replied. "Sgt. Betchel will have our shields if we can't make this bust. He still hasn't forgiven us for the last time we tried to raid the place."

Karen appeared in the backseat of my car, and offered her two cents. "Considering two of his men were killed in that botched attempt, I can understand why he thinks that way."

"Which is why," I added, "we have to make sure all of the bases are covered on this operation. We can't leave anything to chance; our careers are riding on this."

"In that case," Karen stated, "I better keep my mouth shut."

"Why?" my partner quizzed. "Is there something we're missing in all of this?"

The specter observed, "I'm just saying, we know of only three people involved in this transaction. You remember the haul Dryden had in his garage, and Phil said he saw two guys with one cube van. What's not to say there would be more people involved in this exchange?"

Jessica lowered her binoculars. "Karen does have a point, Gary," she said. "Do we have enough reinforcements should more of the Malvern Crew show up?"

"Amerson," I replied, "you saw how many of the Guns and Gangs Unit are here from Toronto. I think we have a good number of officers on this raid."

"Yes," the specter pointed out. "However, remember you thought that way when it was four-on-one, and look what happened."

"I know," I responded. "But, we weren't as prepared for the first raid as we are tonight. I believe we are more equipped tonight for anything that turns up."

We heard a rustling and rumbling of snow and gravel nearby. Jessica grabbed her binoculars and surveyed the situation.

"What you got?" I probed.

"Just as I suspected," she announced. "There's four cube vans coming this way. Better let the Unit know its 'Go Time'."

I got on the CB, and let Base Camp know of the developments. They told us they were at the ready, and awaited my command to strike. Jessica and I took turns peering through our binoculars, and saw about ten men get out of the cube vans. Dryden came out of his dwelling, and talked to a couple of the men for a bit. Then, they moved to the back of one of the vans. Once there, the men opened the rear, and pulled out a few of the weapons they had stowed away in the vehicles. By our observation, they appeared to be of an extremely high-powered variety. I informed the Unit of the situation, and advised them to take caution when approaching the scene. When I saw the men move away from the vans, and towards the garage to load up with the stolen merchandise, I gave the green light to strike.

"Base Camp, Go! Go! Go!" I bellowed.

The Guns and Gangs Unit officers stormed the property, and like we feared, gunfire was exchanged between the two factions. Jessica and I hung low as we joined in the fracas. By the end of it all, one member of the Malvern Crew was gunned down, and a couple others were wounded, as well as, a couple of our forces. However, we were able to round up all eleven individuals, including Dryden, himself. The Guns and Gangs Unit seized all of the weapons and merchandise, and brought them back to Toronto as evidence for the impending case. Plus, as per standard with such a bust, they would be on display for the media when the Unit would hold their press conference to discuss the successful operation.

Jessica and I made our way back to the Detachment once the premises had been swept clean to inform Sgt. Betchel of the successful completion of our mission.

~ * * * ~

When we arrived back at the Detachment in Bewdley, we made a beeline for Sgt. Betchel's office. He was getting ready to call it a night when we knocked on his door.

"Come in," he invited.

Jessica and I walked into his office, and the Sargent shook his head. "I should've known it'd be you two detectives," he scoffed.

"Sorry to have disturbed you so late, sir," I apologized.

"Celdom," he cautioned, "the only way I would be disturbed is if you two came back with bad news about your operation tonight, and I'm hoping this is not the case."

"Negative, Sargent," my partner informed. "We conducted a successful raid tonight, apprehending Dryden and ten members of the Malvern Crew in the process."

The Sargent blinked. "Eleven arrests in the bust? That's incredible! I didn't realize Dryden had that big a connection to the gang scene in Toronto."

"Considering the amount of stolen merchandise he was trying to move," I cited, "he needed a small army to get rid of it."

Jessica and I detailed how the bust went down, noting there were some high-powered weapons to be exchanged for the merchandise. Sgt. Betchel's eyes grew large at the revelation. Had Dryden been successful in obtaining the arms, there would be no telling what kind of havoc he would cause upon the quiet region. However, thanks to our assistance, we were able to nip it in the bud before it came to that.

The Sargent thanked us both for our help on the case, and dismissed us from our commitment to him. We told him it was our pleasure to assist on the matter, and thanked him for the opportunity. Jessica and I left his office, and cleaned out our temporary desks before leaving for my car, and the drive back to my cottage.

CHAPTER 16

Jessica and I walked into my cottage, and collapsed onto my couch. Benny came out to greet us, and I scratched behind his ears. It was our first opportunity to relax since we had arrived earlier in the week. Phil wandered out of his guest room, clad in his traditional bed clothes consisting of a multi-colored sweatshirt and green sleep pants. He ran his fingers through his salt and pepper hair, and appeared groggy from being woken up.

"Did you guys just get in?" he asked.

Jessica nodded. "We just sat down. It's been a long week."

"So, I presume Dryden has been arrested?" the writer queried.

"Affirmative," I confirmed. "He, and ten members of the Malvern Crew, are being shuttled back to Toronto for processing."

Phil turned towards the kitchen. "I'll make some tea, and you can fill me in on the whole bust," he offered.

The writer put the water on, and fetched one of the tins from the cupboard. Jessica and I fought the urge to fall asleep on our friend; however, we were roused awake by the aroma of the blend he selected: an Argentinian yerba mate mixed with coffee beans, white chocolate, and almonds. My partner took one sip, and her eyes shot wide open.

"Jesus, Phil," she complained. "We're trying to relax, not become insomniacs."

"Sorry, Jessica," he apologized. "I thought you two needed a little 'perk-me-up' after the long day you had."

"I'm sure Phil's heart is in the right place," I reasoned, then took a sip of my own cup. Like Jessica, my need to rest my eyes went out the window. "Although," I continued, "his choice of blends could leave something to be desired."

"If you'd like," the writer offered, "I'd fix something else instead."

"No," I corrected. "This will be fine."

"Thanks, Phil," Jessica added.

Phil took a seat across from us, and we recounted the night's proceedings at Dryden's estate. We thanked him again for his tip from earlier in the day, noting it was of great help to us. The writer was quick to correct, stating it was Benny who led him and Maggie to the cottage down the way. Jessica mentioned while Phil figured it would have been only the three individuals making the exchange, there was no way Dryden could have unloaded all of his merchandise with the one cube van he spotted; hence, the need for more gang members to show up at the residence.

"In that case," Phil noted, "it was a good thing you had all of those reinforcements come up from Toronto for the bust. There's no way you two could've taken in all eleven by yourselves."

I agreed. "Especially, after Kassian and Jenner were gunned down by Dryden alone. Yes, there was some blood shed this time around, but it wasn't as devastating as the previous incident up there."

"At least it's all over for now," the writer concluded. "Now, you two can relax for the rest of the week."

"If we can after this tea," Jessica commented. "That's some potent stuff you found in the kitchen there, Phil."

"Ah," I shrugged, "the effects of this will only be for the next little while. We still have two full days up here before we have to head back to Toronto. That still gives us some time to unwind and enjoy Christmas."

Karen appeared in the corner, and decided to change the subject. "Speaking of which," the specter inquired. "What's this I hear about you volunteering to play Santa for a children's party at

Maggie's work?"

"I admit," I added, "I'm curious, too. I thought you weren't one for hanging around little kids."

Phil conceded, "Okay, I'll confess I don't mind most kids. It's only the ones who are yelling, screaming, and being all-around brats that grate on my nerves."

"At a kid's party?" Jessica needled. "You're going to need one hell of a sedative to get through it without blowing your top."

The writer sipped on the last of his tea. "That's already been arranged, Jessica," Phil stated. "Maggie will be there with me. If I want to impress her, I need to be on my best behavior. If that's not incentive enough, I don't know what is?"

The four of us laughed at Phil's comment, and continued to chat for the rest of the night. It was nice to socialize after a difficult case. However, the thing Jessica and I were more interested in, was to see if whether or not Phil could pull off the charade of being 'Jolly Ole St. Nick'.

~ * * * ~

"Come on, Phil," I called out. "Maggie's going to be by any minute."

"Keep your shirt on, Gary," the writer retorted. "I'm getting into costume as fast as I can."

Phil was getting dressed for the children's party he would be performing at with his new companion. It would be an interesting challenge for him, as he had never played such a role before. Yes, he had attended Halloween parties when he was younger, but this was a more festive occasion, and he had a captive audience awaiting him and Maggie to hand out gifts to the younger attendees.

"Do you think he's going to survive the ordeal?" Jessica queried.

"I don't know," I answered. "He claims he will be able to manage it, but if there are any screaming kids there, he might lose his composure, and the illusion will be gone."

"You have to have faith in him," my partner insisted. "I know this is going to be a challenge for Phil, but we'll be there for support. Plus, Maggie will be there alongside of him to keep him in check."

I nodded. "True, he's still trying to win her over, so he needs to be on his best behavior. If he can ace this, it will make him more appealing to her."

"Okay," Phil announced. "I think I'm ready."

The writer closed the door to his room and walked into the living room dressed in full Santa garb, complete with the false beard.

He looked down at his ensemble, and still had he doubts. "I don't know about this, guys," he stated. "I feel like a cross between Father Christmas and a frozen food mascot."

"No," Karen quipped, "if you were going dressed as an elf, you'd look like the mascot."

"That's so reassuring," Phil shot back, sarcastically.

"Stop that, Karen," Jessica scolded the specter before turning her attention to the writer. "You truly look like Santa."

Phil asked, "What do you think, Gary? Do I look like I can pull this off?"

"That depends," I responded. "Can you say the traditional spiel?"

"I'll try." Phil took a deep breath to clear his head, then bellowed, "Ho ho ho! Merry Christmas, everybody!"

"That's perfect," I pronounced.

"I agree," Jessica added. "You've got this, Phil."

"As much as I had my doubts," Karen commented, "I think you can pull this off."

"Don't listen to her, Phil," my partner assured. "You're going to be fine."

The doorbell rang, and I went to answer it. Standing outside with a long winter coat on stood Maggie in her Mrs. Claus outfit.

"Hi, Gary," she replied. "Is my co-star ready for his performance?"

"Come on in, Maggie," I invited. "You can judge for yourself."

My neighbor entered my abode, and upon seeing one another, both Maggie and Phil's faces lit up.

"Well, hello there, Mrs. Claus," Phil beamed. "You look lovely tonight."

Maggie blushed. "Thank you, Santa. Might I say you look majestic in your red suit."

Phil joked, "I have a pair of red long johns on underneath to match."

Karen rolled her eyes, and muttered, "I think we know what's happening after the party tonight."

Jessica quickly interrupted, "Okay, that's enough flirting for now. Remember, you two have to be a respectable First Family of Christmas for the kids."

I agreed. "She's right. Any innuendos and the ilk should be saved for after we get back home. Right now, your audience awaits."

Phil nodded, and offered his arm to Maggie. "Shall we head to the soiree, Mrs. Claus?"

"I would be delighted, Santa," my neighbor giggled.

Kawartha Christmas Caper

The four living members of our ensemble made our way to our vehicles, and began to make our way to the function.

~ * * * ~

The four of us pulled into the parking lot near the university gymnasium, and began to enter the facility. Before entering, Maggie and Phil shirked their coats in the car, and quickly dashed indoors so not to catch frostbite from the bitter cold. Jessica and I trailed behind, but made our way into the main gymnasium where children were running about, and their parents milling around the refreshment tables. Jessica and I began to make our way to grab something to drink, until we heard a commotion near the entrance to the gym. We turned our attention to the entrance to see Maggie and Phil walk in to a round of cheers and shrieks from the children in attendance.

"They look amazing together, don't they?" Jessica asked me.

I nodded. "They do, and not just because they're in their costumes."

'Santa Phil' -- as Jessica and I began to bill him -- took his seat on a majestic throne, and Maggie helped shuttle the children towards him; getting them to sit on his lap, as they told him what they wanted for Christmas. In return, Santa Phil handed them a gift, and a candy cane. On occasion, the couple would pose for a photo with a child. I cringed the odd time when a young child began to wail, as they approached the throne, but much to my surprise, Santa Phil calmed the child down, and made them feel at ease as they had their turn in his lap.

A couple kids came running up to a nearby parent at the refreshment table. "Mommy, Mommy," they yelled. "Look at what Santa gave us."

"That's wonderful," the parent commented. "Did you remember to say 'Thank you' to him?"

"We did," they responded. "And, Mrs. Claus was really nice,

too."

Jessica interjected in the conversation. "That's because you were both really good this year," she stated. "Santa and Mrs. Claus always keep an eye on boys and girls to make sure they get the right gift at this time of year."

The mother whispered to my partner, "I know Mrs. Claus is a colleague of mine here at the university, but do you know who they got to play Santa this year?"

Jessica whispered back, "He's a friend of Maggie MacPhearson's. They needed someone at the last minute, and he volunteered to help out."

"That's a relief. I know they were struggling until the last minute to find someone to fill-in. Do you have any children here at the party?"

"Oh no," Jessica clarified. "We're friends of Santa and Mrs. Claus."

One of the children turned to us. "You're friends with Santa?" they asked. "But, how?"

Without missing a beat, I attempted to make up a story. "I'll let you in on a little secret," I replied. "You know how Santa has helpers up at the North Pole?" The child nodded. I continued, "Well, he has helpers away from there, too. He hires out responsible adults, like police officers, to make sure kids are behaving themselves. That's how he gets his 'Naughty or Nice' list."

The children doubted my claim. "But, you're not a police officer. Where's your uniforms?"

"Not all officers wear uniforms," I explained, then pulled out my badge. "I'm Detective Celdom of the Toronto P.D., and this is my partner, Detective Amerson."

"We were up here for the holidays when duty called us into

action," Jessica added.

The mother worried. "Is everything alright, Detectives?"

Jessica and I looked on at the festivities, and noticed Phil and Maggie enjoying themselves with the children. I replied with a smile, "Everything is fine, ma'am. It's Christmas time."

CHAPTER 17

The sun rose the next morning, and Jessica and I decided to sleep in for a change. It was a good thing neither of us had any children because since it was Christmas morn they would have woken us up at dawn's first light, wanting to open up the bounty Santa had left them. Instead, the only child in our abode was Benny, and like us, he decided to get a later start to the day.

After the party the night before, Phil contemplated about spending the night over at Maggie's; however, he decided to sleep in his room at my cottage instead. He cited while my neighbor's offer was enticing, he thought it was still early in their budding relationship for the two of them to take that step. However, he would later confide to me the notion of falling asleep with someone in his arms was appealing. I guess Phil was a hopeless romantic at heart, and the notion of being involved with someone new for the holidays was the best gift he could ask for.

I dragged my ass out of bed at 9:30 only to find Phil milling about in the kitchen, fixing breakfast for the household.

"Good morning, Gary," the writer greeted. "Merry Christmas."

I stumbled into my seat at the kitchen table. "Merry Christmas to you, too, Phil," I responded. "What time did you get up?"

"About a half hour ago. I figured I'd get up, and fix breakfast for the two of you."

"What about Benny?"

"Oh, I already fed him his kibble, and took him out so he could do his business. It's a little nippy out there, so the cold was a good wake-me-up."

Jessica walked out of her room soon after. "Morning, guys," she said. "Merry Christmas."

"Merry Ho Ho's to you, too, Jessica," Phil commented.

Kawartha Christmas Caper

I kissed my partner. "Merry Christmas, dear," I replied.

Jessica sniffed the air. "Is that bacon I smell?" she inquired.

"It is," Phil confirmed. "I figured I'd treat you both to a traditional Bennett Family Christmas breakfast: toasted bacon sandwiches and 'Christmas coffee'."

I blinked. "'Christmas coffee'?" I quizzed. "Is this some sort of special blend you bought for the holidays?"

"Not really" the writer responded. "It's just regular brewed coffee with an added ingredient."

Phil handed us both steaming mugs of his festive brew, and upon our first sip, we could tell there was something unique about our beverages.

"Are you trying to slip us a mickey?" Jessica accused.

"On the contrary, Jessica," Phil explained. "Whenever I used to spend Christmas at my aunt's, I'd enjoy my Christmas morning coffee with a shot of Irish Cream liqueur in it."

"It's a good thing we're off duty," I noted. "Lt. Davies would have our hides for showing up to work intoxicated."

"I hope Maggie wasn't upset you didn't want to stay over at her place last night," my partner worried.

"She was a little," Phil observed. "But, I did promise I'd drop by later to spend some time with her."

"That will be good of you," I remarked. "It will give you both a chance to spend some of the day together."

"That's my intent," the writer mentioned. "I just hope this long-distance relationship works out better than the last one."

Karen appeared, and offered her two cents on the conversation.

"I don't think it will be a problem," the specter mused. "Amy wasn't mature enough to handle such a relationship. Maggie, on the other hand, appears wise beyond her years."

Phil disputed, "She's not that old, is she?"

The rest of us looked at each other. "Um, Phil," Jessica queried. "How old do you think she is?"

"Closer to my age than Amy was," he answered. "Probably a couple years within mine."

I chuckled. "I hate to break it to you, buddy," I informed. "But, Maggie is five years older than you."

"Quite a switch from the twelve years younger Amy was," Karen noted.

The writer was taken aback. He was now involved with a slightly older woman. While the age difference was not significant to cause tongues to wag from his family members, the notion was something which appealed to him. I don't why it was for some guys to find older women attractive. Personally, I felt age didn't matter when it comes to forming romantic relationships with others, provided the parties involved had obtained the age of majority. I blame a popular series of teen movies which glorified the concept of young men lusting after significantly older women. However, this was not the case with Phil and Maggie. The separation of their birth dates was not as dramatic as they showcased in the movies in question. But, the way I saw it, as long as they liked and respected each other, there was nothing wrong with their new relationship.

We had finished our breakfast when we heard a knock upon my front door. I excused myself from the table to answer it. I opened the door to see Maggie struggling with Biscuit while carrying a load of presents.

"A little help here, please?" she requested.

"Sure thing, Maggie," I answered, grabbing a few of the presents from her arms. "I must admit I'm surprised to see you popping by this morning."

Maggie and Biscuit entered my cottage. "I had bought a few things for you guys to say thanks for everything you've done the past few days."

"Oh, you didn't have to do that. It was our pleasure to help save Christmas for everyone in the area."

"I know, but I wanted to do something nice in return."

"Well, thank you kindly, then."

I placed the presents underneath the tree with the rest of the ones we had already set for the others in my summer abode. Jessica came out from the kitchen, and welcomed my neighbor.

"Merry Christmas, Maggie," my partner greeted.

"Thank you, Jessica," my neighbor replied. "The same to both you and Gary. Is Phil milling about?"

"He's cleaning up in the kitchen after breakfast," I explained. "He was saying he was going to pop by your place later."

"I know he was," Maggie said. "But, I had some gifts to deliver to the two of you, and I figured it would be easier for the six of us to open our presents together."

"That's quite neighborly of you," Jessica noted. "Thank you."

Phil soon entered the fray. "I thought I heard Maggie's voice," he commented. He walked over to his new girlfriend, and kissed her. "Merry Christmas, sweetie."

"Merry Christmas, baby," Maggie responded. "We couldn't wait for you to come over, so we decided to bring Christmas over here."

Phil joked, "This isn't an attempt for you to try to sit in my lap now. I took off the Santa suit when I came home last night."

Maggie playfully smacked the writer's arm. "But, you were so good at the party, I was hoping you could hand out the presents to us all today."

"Come on, Phil," I insisted. "It would be fun."

Jessica added, "Yes, please, Phil?"

Phil resigned himself. "Well," he replied. "If you guys want me to. Just don't expect me to hand out candy canes with them." He turned his attention to Maggie. "But, before I do, would you like some coffee, honey?"

Jessica and I looked at each other when Maggie agreed to have a cup. Fortunately, Karen whispered in his ear, "Make sure to forgo the liqueur with hers. You wouldn't want to be a bad influence on her." Phil nodded, and headed into the kitchen, only to return with a steaming mug of java without the booze for her. Maggie accepted the cup, and thanked him with a kiss.

Once everyone had settled, Phil made his way over to the tree, and began handing out presents to everyone. There were even a couple gifts for Biscuit and Benny, which Maggie and I respectively unwrapped for them.

"Here you go, Jessica and Gary," the writer stated, handing us each a gift. "A little something from me."

"Thank you, Phil," I replied. "But, you shouldn't have."

"Speak for yourself, Gary," my partner scolded, shaking her present to see if it rattled. Alas, it did not.

Both of us unwrapped our presents, and were shocked to discover what they were: bound paperback copies of Phil's first novel.

"Caribbean Crimson by Phil Bennett?" I announced. "You got your book published?"

106

"Self-published," the writer, now author, clarified. "NoMo winners were offered a special code where they could redeem for two free paperback copies of their finished work."

"So, these are available in bookstores?" Jessica queried.

"Not actual brick and mortar stores," Phil explained. "The paperback versions are being sold by a huge online store, but electronic versions are being offered by various retailers."

"I don't know about you," Jessica noted. "But, I'm the type of person who prefers to hold an actual printed copy of a book in their hands."

"I'm the same way," Maggie added. "Although, I admit to not being much of a reader."

Phil gave his girlfriend a look. "And yet," he commented, "you were offering to proofread my future works?"

My neighbor gave her beau a reassuring pat on his hand. "I don't mind doing that, sweetie," she assured. "It's part of my job. But, after reading students' work day after day, I often come home and want to relax by watching TV. That being said, I think your stuff would be more entertaining than a thesis on English literature."

"I hope you do," Phil replied before remembering. "Oh, Gary and Jessica, you might want to turn to the book's title page."

My partner and I opened our books, and were surprised to see our books were personally autographed by the author, himself. The inscription on mine read:

> Gary,
> Thank you for your guidance and inspiration in
> helping me write this book. Your friendship over
> the years means a lot to me. I could not have
> done this without you.
> Phil Bennett

The inscription in my partner's copy was slightly different, but the sentiment was the same. I had to admit, reading the respective personalization of our books touched both Jessica and I. However, I felt bad for Maggie because she appeared to be left out from such a special gift. The feeling subsided when Phil assured her she would receive her own copy in the near future.

Phil resumed handing out gifts to the rest of us, and noticed there was one for him from Maggie. Like Jessica had done earlier, he shook the box to see if it rattled. The difference this time around, it did. Phil carefully unwrapped the present to find a gift box akin to those one would receive from a department store with some clothing in it. He opened the box to find a decorative-bound journal, and a package of ball-point pens.

Maggie explained, "I figured this will help you with your writing."

I agreed, "Especially when you're running low on battery power on your Netbook, and you want to jot down some story ideas."

"This is a wonderful gift," Phil announced. "Thank you ever so kindly, honey." He proceeded to kiss Maggie upon her cheek.

Jessica and I looked on at the happy couple, and uttered a jovial 'Aw!' Phil rolled his eyes at us, but burst out laughing with Maggie soon after. The four of us cuddled with our respective partners, and basked in the festive glow of the holiday morn. My partner turned to me, and had a familiar look in her eyes. It was the same one she had on the night of our first date; a look of love and admiration. With all of the cases Jessica and I had worked on since that night, I had forgotten how much her green eyes sparkled in the light. It was one of the things that made me remember how beautiful she was, and how lucky I was to have her in my life. I smiled back at her, then Phil dangled a sprig of mistletoe above the two of us. Maggie admonished the author for his antics, but I assured her it was alright. Jessica and I leaned in for a soft kiss which made our Christmas complete.

~ * * * ~

After the four of us finished unwrapping our gifts, Benny and Biscuit frolicked around in the piles of discarded wrapping paper. Phil excused himself to make a fresh pot of coffee for us. Once he arrived in the kitchen, a certain ghostly figure was awaiting him.

"This has been quite a holiday," Karen observed, "hasn't it?"

"It certainly has," Phil confirmed. "I had the opportunity to meet a wonderful woman, and start a new relationship with her."

"And," the specter joked, "you met and fell for Maggie, too."

Phil reached for the canister of ground coffee. "You know what I meant."

"I know, but I've given Gary a hard time for years. I can't pass up the opportunity to grind your gears, now that I have the chance."

The author shook his head, and chuckled. "I can see what he saw in you, your rapier wit is endearing."

"Thanks, I try my best."

"The one thing that gets me is how accommodating you've been to Jessica since started dating Gary."

The specter was confused. "What do you mean?"

Phil turned the coffee maker on, and waited for the solution to brew. "I guess I often worried about how Amber felt when I dated Amy. I mean, Amber's spirit wouldn't have approved of the relationship I had with Amy."

"Phil, Amber passed away eleven years before you met Amy. I think she would've wanted you to let go of her, and move on with your life."

"True, but we both know how Amy messed with my head and heart in my relationship. Amber was a kind soul who I absolutely adored, and at one point, I thought Amy would be equal to her. Boy, was I ever wrong there."

"I think with Amy, things moved too fast for her liking, and she wasn't equipped enough to deal with those kind of emotions."

"I see that now. I just don't want to make the same mistakes with Maggie that I did with Amy."

"I don't believe that will be an issue. You're wiser now than you were then, and Maggie is cognizant of your feelings, as well. I think you two are a wonderful match, and I'm thrilled the two of you found each other during this time of year."

Phil smiled. "Thank you, Karen. Say, before you go, could I ask you something?"

"What is it?"

"In your travels in the afterlife, have you ever crossed paths with Amber?"

Karen sighed, and caressed the author's cheek. Then, he felt the presence of another ghostly figure caress the other side of his face.

"Trust me, Phil," Karen replied. "Like I will always be by Gary's side, Amber will always be by yours."

Phil stood there a second as the paranormal energies vanished from the room. He tried his best not to cry, but a couple tears began to seep from his eyes. The author wiped them away, regained his composure, and poured four steaming mugs of freshly brewed coffee before returning to the living room.

CHAPTER 18

After a pleasant and quiet Christmas spent at my cottage, it was time for Jessica, Phil, and I to return to our normal lives back in Toronto. My partner and I were in the process of loading up my car for the two-hour drive to the big city while Phil was saying his goodbyes to my neighbor.

"I hate that you have to go home," Maggie stated.

"Believe me," Phil agreed, "I'm not a fan of it either, but if it's any consolation, there's a bus which connects to the commuter train in Oshawa that goes to Peterborough. If I need a dosage of 'Vitamin M', I could always come up for a weekend."

"I would love that, but that could get a little pricey on a regular basis. How about we conduct online video chats on Sunday mornings instead, with the odd visit up here? It would still give us that connection, without breaking the bank."

Phil nodded. "That would be financially sensible for the time being. At least, until I become flush with royalty payments."

I honked my horn at the couple. "Hey, you two lovebirds," I called out. "It's a long drive back home, and I don't want to get caught in traffic along the 401!"

"Keep your shirt on, Gary," Phil hollered back. "We have to say our proper goodbyes!"

Maggie pouted. "I guess you have to go now," she commented.

"Alas, I do," the author confirmed. "But, I promise I will message you on social media when I get home to let you know I made it alright."

"Please do." Tears began to fall from Maggie's eyes. "I love you, Phil Bennett. I don't want to let you go."

"I love you, too, Maggie MacPhearson. I don't want to let you go either, but I promise, I will stay in touch."

"I'm going to hold you to that." My neighbor and Phil kissed, and gave each other a long embrace that would have gone on forever had I not blared my horn again.

"Alright, already!" Phil yelled at me, before softly telling Maggie he had to go. He kissed her once again, petted Biscuit, and walked over to my car.

Jessica asked my friend, "Are you going to be okay?"

Phil sighed. "I will in due time," he replied. "But, like Shakespeare wrote, 'Parting is such sweet sorrow'."

My partner probed further. "You're crazy about her, aren't you?"

He nodded. "I am. I didn't think I would have seen myself in another relationship, but Maggie and I just clicked."

I mused, "I guess it was a Christmas miracle, of sorts."

Phil thought back to the sensation he felt in my kitchen the previous morning. "More than you know, Gary," he stated. "More than you know."

My friend looked in the rear-view mirror, and saw Karen sitting in the backseat with Benny and Jessica. The specter nodded in affirmation to his comment, which made my partner and I wonder what he alluded to. However, at the time, we didn't pay it any further mind. We waved to Maggie, who was still standing in her doorway, watching us pull onto the roadway. A goodbye honk of my horn blared, and soon, we were heading back home. But, all of us knew, part of Phil was remaining on the shores of Rice Lake after the previous week.

Made in the USA
Columbia, SC
03 September 2022

66607736R00065